Friedrich Schiller, E. M Granger

Schiller's Der Neffe als Onkel

With Footnotes and Vocabulary

Friedrich Schiller, E. M Granger

Schiller's Der Neffe als Onkel
With Footnotes and Vocabulary

ISBN/EAN: 9783743419155

Manufactured in Europe, USA, Canada, Australia, Japa

Cover: Foto ©Andreas Hilbeck / pixelio.de

Manufactured and distributed by brebook publishing software
(www.brebook.com)

Friedrich Schiller, E. M Granger

Schiller's Der Neffe als Onkel

SCHILLER'S

DER NEFFE ALS ONKEL

WITH

FOOTNOTES AND VOCABULARY

Introduction
by
E. M. GRANGER, A.B.

HINDS & NOBLE, PUBLISHERS

4–5–13–14 COOPER INSTITUTE, NEW YORK CITY

Schoolbooks of all publishers at one store

GERMAN

TEXTS

WITH

VOCABULARIES

and explanatory footnotes printed on good paper, bound in cloth, price 50c. per volume. The following texts are now ready: Schiller's Wilhelm Tell, Schiller's Der Neffe als Onkel, Lessing's Minna von Barnhelm, Lessing's Nathan der Weise, and Lessing's Emilia Galotti. Others in preparation.

Sample copies will be sent on approval upon receipt of price. A special discount will be allowed in case of introduction. Correspondence invited.

HINDS & NOBLE

Schoolbooks of All Publishers at One Store

4-5-13-14 Cooper Institute, New York City

INTRODUCTION.

I. SKETCH OF SCHILLER'S LIFE.

JOHANN CHRISTOPH FRIEDRICH SCHILLER, the beloved poet of Germany, the singer of liberty, the admired and admiring friend of Goethe, was born at Marbach, in Würtemberg, November 10th, 1759. His father was an army surgeon under the Duke of Würtemberg, being in service during the war of the Austrian Succession and also during the Seven Years' War. He afterward held small military positions in different places, but under the same authority. Schiller's mother was Elisabetha Dorothea Kodweis, daughter of a baker and innkeeper. The circumstances of Schiller's parents were always poor during his youth, so that in their actions they were largely dependent upon the wishes of the reigning duke. Thus it was that while Schiller was yet a child the family moved to Lorch, and in 1766 to Ludwigsburg, where they finally settled. At Lorch the child received his first lessons from Moser, the aged pastor, and at Ludwigsburg he was entered in the grammar school. From his first teacher he imbibed a desire to become a clergyman, and his parents were in sympathy with this wish; but the duke, Karl Eugen, was establishing a military academy at Stuttgart, and wanted pupils, so, in spite of the protests of his father, Schiller was compelled to become a student there, while in his fourteenth year.

The duke's command was in the form of an offer of a free education, but in return the father signed a bond which put Schiller's services and career into the duke's hands. He entered first as a law student, and then as a medical student. The discipline in the school was very severe, but Schiller found time, amid his uncongenial surroundings and occupations, to read the works of poets and philosophers and to try his own hand at writing. His first production of moment was the "Robbers." This was printed at his own expense, in July, 1781, although it had been begun before the writer was nineteen. The play was performed at Mannheim the next winter with great success, and Schiller was present to enjoy it. Some months later he visited Mannheim again for the same purpose, but on his return was arrested for breach of discipline. He was at this time regimental surgeon, but shortly after his second visit to Mannheim, the magistrates of the Swiss canton of the Grisons complained of a passage in the "Robbers," and the duke forbade Schiller writing. The poet thereupon left Stuttgart secretly, and after a fruitless visit to Mannheim and to Frankfort, he settled for some months at Bauerbach, near Meiningen, the summer home of Frau von Wolzogen, mother of some student friends. Here he finished "Fiesco," already begun, and wrote "Plot and Passion." In 1783 he returned to Mannheim, where he obtained the position of poet to the theatre, which gave him a moderate income. He remained there in comparative comfort for about a year, then having given up his position, he went to Leipzig. Before leaving Mannheim,

Schiller began the publication of the *Rheinische Thalia*, devoted to the drama, dramatic criticisms, discussions, etc. He continued this periodical until 1794. Part of "Don Carlos" appeared in its first number, but the entire play was not published until 1786, when he was living in Dresden with Christian Gottfried Körner, his devoted friend and admirer. In Dresden he wrote part of a novel called the "Geisterseher," and becoming deeply interested in the subject of history, began his "Revolt of the Netherlands," the first volume of which appeared in 1788. In 1787 Schiller first went to Weimar, where he met Herder and Wieland, who immediately became his friends. About this time he made the acquaintance of Fräulein Charlotte von Lengefeld, whom he married February 22d, 1790. The marriage was very happy, and Schiller's wife proved both a help and a comfort to him. In 1789 he became professor of history at the University of Jena, which is near Weimar, and where he was able to enjoy the friendship of other men of letters, Goethe being the foremost. The friendship of these two poets, slow to begin, became firm and lasting, each inspiring the other, and no finer tribute has been paid to Schiller than that made by Goethe after the former's death.

The poet had now a small salary and an equal pension from Karl August, so that he could live in modest ease. His first complete historical work was the "History of the Thirty Years' War." While still at work on this book he fell ill, and his position would have been very hard, but the Prince of Holstein-Augustenburg and Count von Schimmelmann together granted him an annual pension of one thousand thalers for three years.

Schiller rested, visited his parents in his old home, and partially recovered his health. On his return to Jena, he started, in company with Goethe, the *Horen*, which covered a greater range of subjects than the *Thalia*, now discontinued. Some of Schiller's finest essays and poems appeared in the *Horen*, and some of his best short poems were first published in the *Musen-Almanach*, started about the same time. The latter also contained the "Xenien," a series of epigrams written by both the poets, and the result of jealousy and ill-will on the part of other authors.

In 1799 appeared "Wallenstein," a tragedy in three parts, on which Schiller had been working for seven years. This drama, the subject of which had suggested itself to him during his labors on the "History of the Thirty Years' War," was the greatest he had yet produced; Carlyle calls it the greatest dramatic work of the eighteenth century.

Immediately after the completion of "Wallenstein" Schiller began studying for "Mary Stuart," his next play. But before this was produced, his "Song of the Bell" appeared. This was always his most popular poem, and sank deep into the German heart.

Toward the end of this same year Schiller moved with his family into Weimar, where he spent the rest of his short life. From this time on he received a yearly pension from the Grand Duke, which made his circumstances easier, and he soon had a home of his own, where he worked and studied, and where his friends often met.

"Mary Stuart" was brought out in 1800, but was not so successful as some of Schiller's other plays. In 1801 appeared the "Maid of Orleans," which was received with great enthusiasm. This play is beautiful and in many ways great, but it presents an idealized maid, and not the simple peasant girl.

The poet's next play was the " Bride of Messina" (1803), a tragedy constructed on the lines of the old Greek drama, including the chorus. Schiller's leanings had long been growing in this direction, and he hoped much from this play. But the classic form, austere and artificial, won no welcome from the modern audience, and Schiller made no further attempt therein.

The next year his last and greatest play was produced. This was "William Tell." Shortly after its completion the poet made a visit to Berlin, and before reaching his home again was suddenly taken ill. He partially recovered, but in the spring he again became worse, and died May 9th, 1805, aged somewhat over forty-five years.

In appearance Schiller was tall and quite lean, with dark-red hair, a pale, thin face, and thoughtful and dreamy eyes, which lighted up when he became enthusiastic. Carlyle says: "To judge from his portraits, Schiller's face expressed well the features of his mind: it is mildness tempering strength; fiery ardor shining through the clouds of suffering and disappointment, deeply but patiently endured. . . . There are few faces that affect us more than Schiller's; it is at once meek, tender, unpretending, and heroic."

The judgment of to-day does not give Schiller's genius so high a place as that of his own age; nevertheless, it is not to be denied that he did much to advance German literature. His works will always be read as forming a notable part of his country's thought, and the people of Germany will always love and admire both the man and his writings. He began by preaching revolt in the

"Robbers," and ended by singing of liberty in "William Tell." Liberty was always his gospel, but its stormy expression in youth gave place to a calmer but no less earnest appeal in later life. In character Schiller was what a close student of his works and actions will judge him to be, at once eager and tender, changeful yet always persevering, industrious beyond expectation, in spite of ill health, in his chosen work, modest and unassuming in his tastes, yet in many of his ideas lofty and, according to Goethe, aristocratic; but the characteristic that is above all insisted upon by those who knew him was his "inexhaustible cheerfulness." He was courageous and hopeful to an unusual degree; and it is pleasant to be able to say with Carlyle: "On the whole, we may pronounce him happy."

II. "THE NEPHEW AS UNCLE."

As is well known, this play was not original with Schiller, but was an adaptation from the French of Louis Benoit Picard, whose plays were having much vogue at that time. The work was begun at the suggestion of Duke Karl August of Weimar, who wished to see some of the contemporary French plays on the German stage. Besides this one (called "Encore des Mènechmes" in the original) Schiller adapted one other of Picard's—"Médiocre et Rampant, ou Le Moyen de Parvenir"—which, originally written in Alexandrine verse, Schiller translated into prose as "The Parasite."

"The Nephew as Uncle" was already in prose in the original, but Schiller changed the *dramatis personæ* and much of the dialogue. Schiller himself calls it "a light play of intrigue "; its plot, as is indicated by its French title, was itself an adaptation from the "Menæchmi" of Plautus, and hinges on the likeness of appearance between two people. The comedy was written between February and May, 1803, its first performance in Weimar being upon the 18th of the latter month. It was well received and became quite popular.

The story briefly told is as follows: Young *Dorsigny*, who closely resembles his uncle, has fought a duel and appears at the uncle's residence for the purpose of hiding, a wig and change of uniform having made the resemblance complete. His sister meets him and tells him that his cousin *Sophie*, whom he loves, is to marry young *Lormeuil* when her father, *Colonel Dorsigny*, returns. Young *Dorsigny*, personating his uncle, gives *Sophie* consent to marry himself. But while they are preparing for an immediate marriage, *Colonel Dorsigny* returns unexpectedly with young *Lormeuil*. When he meets with the results of his nephew's plans, of which he is entirely ignorant, the scenes are exceedingly laughable. Young *Lormeuil* himself, the prospective bridegroom, finds the key to the riddle, and as he has fallen in love at first sight with the sister of young *Dorsigny*, he very willingly yields *Sophie* to her cousin and accepts another bride for himself.

It will be seen that the plot is very slight and that the effect of the play lies entirely in the situations. The constant confusion of uncle and nephew until they are finally brought face to face furnishes opportunity for that genuine humor of which the theatre-going public never tires and which likewise makes pleasant reading.

Perſonen[1].

Oberſt von[2] Dorſigny.
Frau von Dorſigny.
Sophie, ihre Tochter.
Franz von Dorſigny, ihr Neffe.
Frau von Mirville, ihre Nichte.
Cormeuil, Sophiens Bräutigam[3].
Dalcour, Freund des[4] jungen Dorſigny.
Champagne, Bedienter des jungen Dorſigny.
Ein Notar.
Zwei Unteroffiziere[5].
Ein Poſtillon.
Jasmin, Diener in Dorſignys Hauſe.
Drei Lakaien.

Die Scene iſt ein Saal mit einer Thür im Fond[6], die zu einem Garten führt[7]. Auf beiden Seiten ſind Kabinettsthüren[8].

---

1. the persons of the play (Dramatis Personae). 2. French names usually keep their French titles; as, colonel de Dorsigny, Madame de Mirville etc. 3. intended; betrothed. 4. of. 5. sergeants; non-commissioned officers in the army. 6. at the back. 7. leading into; opening on . . . . 8. doors.

NB. Bei der Überſetzung beachte man, daß das häufig im emphatiſchen Sinne vorkommende „ja" durch „why", „to be sure", „indeed" und ähnliche Ausdrücke wiederzugeben iſt.

Erster Aufzug.

Erster Auftritt.

Dalcour (tritt eilfertig herein, und nachdem er sich überall umgesehen[1], ob niemand[2] zugegen, tritt er zu einem von den Wachs=lichtern, die vorn auf einem Schreibtisch brennen, und liest ein Billet). „Herr von Balcour wird ersucht[3], diesen Abend um sechs „Uhr sich im Gartensaal des Herrn von Dorsigny einzu= „finden[4]. Er kann zu[5] dem kleinen Pförtchen hereinkommen, „das den ganzen Tag offen ist." — Keine Unterschrift! — Hm! Hm! ein seltsames Abenteuer. — Ist's vielleicht[6] eine hübsche Frau, die mir hier ein Rendezvous geben will?[7] — Das wäre[8] allerliebst. — Aber still[9]! Wer sind die beiden Figuren, die eben da eintreten, wo[10] ich hereingekommen bin?

Zweiter Auftritt.

Franz von Dorsigny und **Champagne** (beide in Mäntel eingewickelt). **Dalcour.**

Dorsigny (seinen Mantel an Champagne gebend). Ei[11] guten Abend, lieber Balcour[12]!

Dalcour. Was? Bist du's[13], Dorsigny? Wie kommst du hieher[14]? Und wozu diese sonderbare Aus= staffierung[15] — diese Perücke und diese Uniform, die nicht von[16] deinem Regiment ist?

---

1. after looking all round. 2. to see if any one. 3. is re-quested. 4. to repair to the drawing room of M. de D.'s summer-residence. 5. by. 6. perhaps it is. 7. who wants to meet me here. 8. that would be. 9. hush. 10. who are just entering by the same gate where I did. 11. aha. 12. my dear V. 13. is it you. 14. what makes you come here. 15. odd equipment; strange disguise. 16. which is not that of . . . .

1*

Dorsigny. Meiner Sicherheit wegen[1]. — Ich habe mich mit meinem Oberstlieutenant geschlagen[2]; er ist schwer verwundet, und ich komme, mich in Paris zu verbergen[3]. Weil man mich aber in meiner eigenen Uniform gar zu leicht erkennt[4], so habe ich's fürs sicherste gehalten[5], das Kostüm meines Onkels anzunehmen[6]. Wir sind so ziemlich von einem Alter[7], wie du weißt und einander an Gestalt, an Größe, an Farbe, bis zum Verwechseln ähnlich[8] und führen überdies noch einerlei Namen. Der einzige Unterschied ist, daß der Oberst eine Perücke trägt und ich meine eigenen Haare. — Jetzt aber, seitdem ich mir seine Perücke und die Uniform seines Regiments zulegte, erstaune ich selbst über die große Ähnlichkeit mit ihm[9]. In diesem Augenblick komme ich an[10] und bin erfreut, dich so pünktlich bei dem Rendezvous zu finden.

Valcour. Bei dem Rendezvous? Wie? Hat sie dir auch etwas davon vertraut?[11]

Dorsigny. Wie? Welche sie[12]?

Valcour. Nun[13], die hübsche Dame, die mich in einem Billet hierher beschieden[14]. Du bist mein Freund, Dorsigny, und ich habe nichts Geheimes vor[15] dir.

Dorsigny. Die allerliebste Dame!

Valcour. Worüber lachst du[16]?

Dorsigny. Ich bin die schöne Dame, Valcour.

---

1. for safety's sake; for my own safety. 2. I've had a duel with . . . 3. and I've come to Paris to hide myself there. 4. but as I should have been much too easily recognised . . . . 5. I've deemed (considered) it (the) safest (plan). 6. to put on. 7. we are pretty much of the same age. 8. to resemble one another in appearance . . . . so as to be easily mistaken one for the other. 9. I'm myself astonished at our . . . . 10. I've this moment arrived. 11. has she made a confidant of you, too; has she taken you, too, into her confidence? 12. she, which she. 13. why. 14. who wrote me a note to say that she wished to meet me here. 15. I have no secrets from. 16. what are you laughing at.

Dalcour. Du?

Dorſigny. Das Billet iſt von mir.

Dalcour. Ein ſchönes Quiproquo, zum Teufel[1]! — Was fällt dir aber ein, deine Briefe nicht zu unterzeichnen[2]? Leute von meinem Schlag[3] können ſich bei ſolchen Billets auf etwas ganz anders Rechnung machen[4]. — Aber da es ſo ſteht, gut[5]! Wir nehmen einander nichts übel[6], Dorſigny. — Alſo[7] ich bin dein gehorſamer Diener.

Dorſigny. Warte doch[8]! Warum eilſt du ſo hin= weg? Es lag mir viel daran[9], dich zu ſprechen, ehe ich mich vor jemand anderem ſehen ließ[10]. Ich brauche deines Beiſtandes; wir müſſen Abrede miteinander nehmen.

Dalcour. Gut. — Du kannſt auf mich zählen; aber jetzt laß mich[11], ich habe dringende Geſchäfte.

Dorſigny. So! Jetzt, da du mir einen Dienſt erzeigen ſollſt?[12] — Aber zu einem galanten Abenteuer hatteſt du Zeit übrig[13].

Dalcour. Das nicht[14], lieber Dorſigny! Aber ich muß fort[15]; man erwartet mich[16].

Dorſigny. Wo?

Dalcour. Beim l'Hombre.

Dorſigny. Die große Angelegenheit[17]!

Dalcour. Scherz beiſeite[18]. Ich habe dort Ge=

---

1. a pretty sell, confound it. 2. but why on earth don't you sign your letters. 3. gentlemen like me. 4. naturally expect something quite different from ... 5. but since the matter stands thus, all right. 6. we won't be offended at it; we won't be angry with one another; we'll take it all in good part. 7. so. 8. one moment, if you please. 9. I've been very anxious; it is of the utmost importance to me. 10. before showing myself to any other person; before allowing anybody else to see me. 11. excuse me. 12. you are to .... 13. you had plenty of time (time to spare). 14. not exactly. 15. I must be off. 16. I've an engagement. 17. the all engrossing business, of course. 18. joking apart; with- out any joking; in real earnest.

legenheit, die Schwester deines Oberstlieutenants zu sehen. — Sie hält was auf mich[1]; ich will dir bei ihr das Wort reden[2].

Dorsigny. Nun meinetwegen[3]. Aber thu mir den Gefallen, meine Schwester, die Frau von Mirville, im Vorbeigehen[4] wissen zu lassen, daß man sie hier im Gartensaal erwarte[5]. — Nenne mich aber nicht, hörst du[6]?

Dalcour. Da sei außer Sorgen[7]! Ich habe keine Zeit dazu und will es ihr hinauf sagen lassen[8], ohne sie nur einmal zu sehen[9]. Übrigens behalte ich mir's vor, bei einer andern Gelegenheit ihre nähere Bekanntschaft zu machen[10]. Ich schätze den Bruder zu sehr, um die Schwester nicht zu lieben, wenn sie hübsch ist, versteht sich[11]. (ab.)

Dritter Auftritt.

Dorsigny. Champagne.

Dorsigny. Zum Glück brauche ich seinen Beistand sogar nötig nicht[12]. — Es ist mir weniger um das Verbergen zu thun[13] (denn vielleicht fällt es niemand ein[14]), mich zu verfolgen), als um meine liebe Cousine Sophie wiederzusehen.

Champagne. Was Sie für ein glücklicher Mann sind, gnädiger Herr[15]! — Sie sehen Ihre Geliebte[16] wieder

---

1. she has a pretty good opinion of me; she has some regard for me. 2. I'll speak to her in your behalf. 3. well, as you like. 4. in passing; by the way. 5. that somebody is waiting for her in the summer-house (in the pavilion). 6. but don't mention my name, d'ye hear (do you hear). 7. no fear on that score; make your mind easy about that. 8. I will send up word to her. 9. without as much as (even) seeing her. 10. I reserve to myself for another occasion the pleasure of making ... 11. of course. 12. I don't stand so particularly in need of (I don't so very much require) his assistance. 13. it is of less importance to me to hide myself. 14. for nobody, perhaps, dreams (will think) of ... 15. how lucky you are, sir; how happy is your honour's lot. 16. your love.

und ich (seufzt) meine Frau! Wann geht's wieder zurück
ins¹ Elsaß? — wir lebten wie die Engel, da wir fünfzig
Meilen weit voneinander waren².

Dorsigny. Still! Da kommt meine Schwester!

Vierter Auftritt.
Vorige. Frau von Mirville.

Fr. v. Mirville. Ah! Sind Sie es? Sei'n Sie
von Herzen willkommen³!

Dorsigny. Nun, das ist doch⁴ ein herzlicher Empfang!

Fr. v. Mirville. Das ist [ja] recht schön⁵, daß Sie
uns so überraschen⁶! Sie schrieben, daß Sie eine lange
Reise vorhätten⁷, von der Sie frühestens⁸ in einem Monat
zurück sein könnten, und vier Tage darauf sind Sie hier?

Dorsigny. Geschrieben hätt' ich und an wen⁹?

Fr. v. Mirville. An meine Tante! (Sieht [den] Champagne, der seinen Mantel ablegt). Wo ist denn aber Herr von
Lormeuil?

Dorsigny. Wer ist der Herr von Lormeuil?

Fr. v. Mirville. Ihr künftiger Schwiegersohn.

Dorsigny. Sage mir, für wen hältst du mich¹⁰?

Fr. v. Mirville. Nun, doch wohl¹¹ für meinen
Onkel!

Dorsigny. Ist's möglich! Meine Schwester erkennt
mich nicht!

Fr. v. Mirville. Schwester? Sie — mein Bruder?

Dorsigny. Ich — dein Bruder.

---

1. when are we to (shall we) return to. 2. we were as
happy as angels, whilst living fifty miles apart from one another. 3. you are heartily welcome. 4. I must say; really; indeed.
5. it's very nice of you. 6. to take us thus by surprise. 7. that
you intended going on . . . 8. at the (very) earliest. 9. did I,
and to whom. 10. whom do you take me for. 11. of course.

Fr. v. Mirville. Das kann nicht sein. Das ist nicht möglich. Mein Bruder ist bei[1] seinem Regiment zu Straßburg, mein Bruder trägt sein eigenes Haar, und das ist auch seine Uniform nicht[2] — und so groß auch sonst die Ähnlichkeit[3] —

Dorsigny. Eine Ehrensache, die aber sonst nicht viel zu bedeuten haben wird[4], hat mich genötigt, meine Garnison in aller Geschwindigkeit zu verlassen; um nicht erkannt zu werden[5], steckte ich mich in[6] diesen Rock und diese Perücke.

Fr. v. Mirville. Ist's möglich? — O so laß dich herzlich umarmen[7], lieber Bruder. — Ja, nun fange ich an, dich zu erkennen! Aber die Ähnlichkeit ist doch ganz erstaunlich.

Dorsigny. Mein Onkel ist also abwesend?

Fr. v. Mirville. Freilich, der Heirat wegen.

Dorsigny. Der Heirat? — Welcher[8] Heirat?

Fr. v. Mirville. Sophiens, meiner Cousine[9].

Dorsigny. Was hör' ich, Sophie soll heiraten[10]?

Fr. v. Mirville. Ei freilich[11]! Weißt du es denn nicht[12]?

Dorsigny. Mein Gott! Nein[13]!

Champagne (nähert sich). Nicht ein Wort wissen wir[14].

Fr. v. Mirville. Herr von Lormeuil, ein alter Kriegskamerad des Onkels[15], der zu Toulon wohnt, hat für seinen Sohn um Sophien angehalten[16]. — Der junge Lor=

---

1. with.   2. nor is this his uniform; and moreover (besides), this is not . . .   3. great as the resemblance otherwise is.   4. which, however, is not likely to be of great consequence.   5. in order to avoid being recognised; in order not to be recognised.   6. I put on.   7. oh, then let me embrace you heartily.   8. which.   9. my cousin Sophy's (marriage).   10. Sophia is going to be married.   11. to be sure, she is.   12. didn't you know.   13. good gracious! no, I didn't.   14. we haven't the faintest knowledge of it.   15. an old brother officer of uncle's.   16. has asked Sophia in marriage for his son.

meuil foll ein fehr liebenswürdiger Mann fein, fagt man[1];
wir haben ihn noch nicht gefehen. Der Onkel holt ihn zu
Toulon ab[2]; dann wollen fie eine weite Reife zufammen
machen[3], um ich weiß nicht welche Erbfchaft in Befitz zu
nehmen[4]. In einem Monat benken fie[5] zurück zu fein, und
wenn du alsdann noch da bift, fo kannft du zur Hochzeit
mit tanzen.

Dorfigny. Ach, liebe Schwefter! — Redlicher Cham=
pagne! Ratet, helft mir! Wenn ihr mir nicht beifteht, fo
ift es aus mit mir[6], fo bin ich verloren.

Fr. v. Mirville. Was haft du denn[7], Bruder?
Was ift dir[8]?

Champagne. Mein Herr ift verliebt in feine Coufine.

Fr. v. Mirville. Ah, ift es das!

Dorfigny. Diefe unglückfelige[9] Heirat darf nun und
nimmermehr zu ftand kommen[10].

Fr. v. Mirville. Es wird fchwer halten[11], fie rück=
gängig zu machen. Beide Väter find einig[12], das Wort ift
gegeben, die Artikel find aufgefetzt[13], und man erwartet
bloß noch den Bräutigam, fie zu unterzeichnen und ab=
zufchließen.

Champagne. Geduld! — Hören Sie[14]! (Tritt zwifchen
beide). Ich habe einen fublimen Einfall!

Dorfigny. Rede!

Champagne. Sie haben einmal[15] den Anfang ge=

---

1. they say young L. is a very nice gentleman. 2. uncle has
arranged to meet him at T. 3. they then intend taking a long
journey together. 4. in order to take possession of some inheritance or other. 5. they expect (intend). 6. it is all up with me.
7. what is the matter with you. 8. what ails you. 9. ill-fated;
ill-starred. 10. must never take place. 11. it will be rather
difficult; it won't be at all an easy matter. 12. agreed. 13. the
marriage-articles are (the marriage-contract is) drawn up. 14. listen.
15. now.

macht, Ihren Onkel vorzustellen! Bleiben Sie dabei[1]! Führen Sie die Rolle durch[2].

Fr. v. Mirville. Ein schönes Mittel, um die Nichte zu heiraten.

Champagne. Nur gemach! Lassen Sie mich meinen Plan entwickeln. — Sie spielen [also] Ihren Onkel! Sie sind [nun] Herr hier im Hause, und Ihr erstes Geschäft ist, die bewußte Heirat wieder aufzuheben[3]. — Sie haben den jungen Lormeuil nicht mitbringen können[4], weil er — weil er gestorben ist. — Unterdessen erhält Frau v. Dorsigny einen Brief von Ihnen, als dem Neffen[5], worin Sie um die Cousine anhalten. — Das ist mein Amt! Ich bin der Kurier, der den Brief von Straßburg bringt. — Frau v. Dorsigny ist verliebt in[6] ihren Neffen, sie nimmt diesen Vorschlag mit der besten Art von der Welt auf[7]; sie teilt ihn Ihnen als ihrem Eheherrn mit[8], und Sie lassen sich's wie billig, gefallen[9]. Nun stellen Sie sich, als wenn Sie aufs eiligste verreisen müßten[10]; Sie geben der Tante unbedingte Vollmacht[11], diese Sache zu Ende zu bringen. Sie reisen ab, und den andern Tag[12] erscheinen Sie in Ihren natürlichen Haaren und in der Uniform Ihres Regiments wieder, als wenn Sie eben spornstreichs von Ihrer Garnison herkämen[13]. Die Heirat geht vor sich[14]; der Onkel kommt stattlich angezogen[15] mit seinem Bräutigam, der den

---

1. stick to it; continue to do so. 2. play the part through. 3. to countermand (to break off) the marriage in question. 4. you were unable to bring L. with you. 5. as her nephew. 6. dotes on ...; is dotingly fond of ... 7. she receives (accepts, entertains, agrees to) this proposal with the best grace in the world. 8. she imparts it to you ... 9. you agree to it, (you don't object to it) of course; you are, of course, perfectly satisfied with it. 10. to be obliged to start off (to depart, to set out) instantly. 11. ample authority and full power. 12. next day; the day after. 13. as though you had just arrived at full speed from your garrison town. 14. takes place. 15. arrives in state.

Platz glücklich[1] besetzt findet, und nichts Bessers zu thun hat, als umzukehren und sich entweder zu Toulon oder in Ostindien eine Frau zu holen[2].

Dorsigny. Glaubst du, mein Onkel werde das so geduldig —

Champagne. O er wird aufbrausen, das versteht sich[3]! Es wird heiß werden am Anfang[4]. — Aber er liebt Sie[5]! er liebt seine Tochter! Sie geben ihm die besten Worte[6], versprechen ihm eine Stube voll artiger Enkelchen, die ihm alle so ähnlich sehen sollen, wie Sie selbst[7]. Er lacht, er besänftigt sich[8], und alles ist vergessen.

Fr. v. Mirville. Ich weiß nicht, ist es das Tolle dieses Einfalls[9], aber er fängt an, mich zu reizen[10].

Champagne. O er ist himmlisch, der Einfall.

Dorsigny. Lustig genug ist er, aber nur nicht aus= führbar — meine Tante wird mich wohl für den Onkel ansehen[11]!

Fr. v. Mirville. Habe ich's doch[12]!

Dorsigny. Ja, im ersten Augenblicke[13].

Fr. v. Mirville. Wir müssen ihr keine Zeit lassen[14], aus der Täuschung zu kommen[15]. Wenn wir die Zeit be= nutzen[16], [so] brauchen wir auch nur einen Augenblick[17].

---

1. successfully.   2. and to get a wife at T. or in the E. I. 3. he will fly into a violent passion, of course.   4. it will be hot work at first.   5. he likes (is fond of) you.   6. you coax and caress him; you flatter and cajole him; (you treat him to any amount of soft sawder; *slang*, aber im Munde des Bedienten ganz am Platze).   7. who shall all be as like him as you are yourself. 8. his anger is appeased (soothed, assuaged).   9. whether it is the extravagance of this idea.   10. I begin to like it; it begins to please (tickle) me.   11. isn't likely to take me for ...   12. didn't I.   13. at first sight.   14. we must not allow her any time.   15. to discover the trick (the deception).   16. if we make the most of the (our) time; if we turn our time to the best advantage.   17. a moment is all we want.

— Es ist jetzt Abend, die Dunkelheit kommt uns zu statten[1]; diese Lichter leuchten nicht hell genug[2], um den Unterschied bemerklich[3] zu machen. Den Tag brauchst du gar nicht zu erwarten[4] — du erklärst zugleich, daß du in der Nacht[5] wieder fortreisen müssest, und morgen erscheinst du in deiner wahren Person. Geschwind ans Werk[6]! Wir haben keine Zeit zu verlieren — Schreibe den Brief an unsre Tante, den dein Champagne als Kurier überbringen soll[7], und worin du um Sophien anhältst.

Dorsigny (an den Schreibtisch gehend). Schwester! Schwester! Du machst mit mir, was du willst[8].

Champagne (sich die Hand reibend)[9]. Wie freue ich mich über[10] meinen klugen Einfall! Schade, daß ich schon eine Frau habe, ich könnte[11] hier eine Hauptrolle spielen, anstatt [jetzt] bloß den Vertrauten zu machen[12].

Fr. v. Mirville. Wie das[13], Champagne?

Champagne. Ei nun[14], das ist ganz natürlich. Mein Herr gilt für[15] seinen Onkel, ich würde den Herrn von Lormeuil vorstellen, und wer weiß, was mir am Ende nicht noch blühen könnte[16], wenn meine verdammte Heirat —

Fr. v. Mirville. Wahrhaftig[17], meine Cousine hat Ursache, sich darüber zu betrüben[18]!

---

1. the darkness will favour us (will be our ally). 2. don't give sufficient light. 3. easily noticed. 4. there is not the slightest occasion (it is not at all necessary) to wait for . . . 5. this very night. 6. look sharp; quick to your work. 7. is to. 8. you do with me as (whatever) you please (like). 9. rubbing his hands. 10. how rejoiced (delighted) I am at . . . 11. I might. 12. instead of being merely . . . 13. how so. 14. why. 15. passes for. 16. what good fortune might yet be in store for me; what piece of good luck might yet fall to my share. 17. really; upon my word. 18. to be grieved at it; to regret it deeply; to lament (to deplore) it sincerely.

Dorsigny (siegelt den Brief und gibt ihn an Champagne).
Hier ist der Brief. Richt' es nun ein, wie du willst! Dir überlaß' ich mich[1].

Champagne. Sie sollen[2] mit mir zufrieden sein. — In wenigen Augenblicken[3] werde ich damit als Kurier von Straßburg ankommen, gespornt und gestiefelt, triefend von Schweiß[4]. — Sie, gnädiger Herr, halten sich wacker[5]. — Mut, Dreistigkeit, Unverschämtheit, wenn's nötig ist[6]. — Den Onkel gespielt[7], die Tante angeführt, die Nichte geheiratet, und wenn alles vorbei ist, den Beutel gezogen[8] und den redlichen Diener gut bezahlt[9], der Ihnen zu allen diesen Herrlichkeiten verholfen hat[10].

(ab.)

Fr. v. Mirville. Da kommt die Tante. Sie wird dich für den Onkel ansehen. Thu, als wenn du notwendig mit ihr zu reden hättest[11] und schick' mich weg.

Dorsigny. Aber was werd' ich ihr denn sagen[12])?

Fr. v. Mirville. Alles, was ein galanter Mann seiner Frau nur Artiges sagen kann[13].

---

1. I put myself entirely in your hands. 2. you shall .... 3. in a very short time; (in a jiffy; *slang*, aber im Munde des Bedienten am Platze). 4. in a state of great perspiration. 5. keep up your courage. 6. if need be. 7. gespielt, angeführt, geheiratet, gezogen, bezahlt sind durch Imperative zu übersetzen: personate the uncle, deceive the aunt u. s. w. 8. pull out your purse; out with your purse. 9. pay handsomely; (and when all is over, out with your purse and down with your dust (cash, money) to reward handsomely the honest servant ... *slang*, aber der Sprache des Champagne angemessen). 10. who has procured for you all this happiness. 11. as if you particularly wanted to tell her something; as if you had something particular to tell her. 12. what shall I say to her. 13. all the pretty things an attentive (polite, courteous) husband can say to his wife; all the compliments that a gallant husband can pay to his wife. (gallant hat den Ton auf der zweiten Silbe).

Fünfter Auftritt.

**Frau von Mirville. Frau von Dorsigny.
Franz von Dorsigny.**

Fr. v. Mirville. Kommen Sie doch[1], liebe Tante! Geschwind! Der Onkel ist angekommen.

Fr. v. Dorsigny. Wie? Was? Mein Mann? — Ja wahrhaftig, da ist er! — Herzlich willkommen, lieber Dorsigny! — So bald erwartete[2] ich Sie nicht. — Nun! Sie haben doch[3] eine glückliche Reise gehabt? — Aber wie so allein[4]? Wo sind Ihre Leute? Ich hörte doch Ihre Kutsche nicht — nun wahrhaftig — ich besinne mich kaum[5] — ich zittre vor[6] Überraschung und Freude —

Fr. v. Mirville (heimlich[7] zu ihrem Bruder). Nun, [so] rede doch[8]! Antworte frischweg[9]!

Dorsigny. Weil ich nur auf einen kurzen Besuch ·hier bin, so komm ich allein und in einer Mietkutsche[10]. — Was aber die Reise betrifft[11], liebe Frau[12] — die Reise — ach! die ist nicht die glücklichste gewesen.

Fr. v. Dorsigny. Sie erschrecken mich! — Es ist Ihnen doch kein Unglück zugestoßen[13]?

Dorsigny. Nicht eben mir! mir nicht[14]! — Aber diese Heirat — (zur Frau von Mirville) Liebe Nichte, ich habe mit der Tante —[15]

Fr. v. Mirville. Ich will nicht stören, mein Onkel[16].

(ab.)

---

1. come, please; do come, pray. 2. to expect. 3. I hope. 4. but why (are you) quite alone. 5. I'm scarcely able to collect my thoughts. 6. with. 7. low; softly. 8. now, do say something, please. 9. answer·her boldly; speak to her frankly. 10. I've come alone, and in a hackney-coach, because I can stay here but a very short time. 11. as for the journey; as regards the journey. 12. my dear. 13. no accident has happened to you, I hope; no mishap has befallen you, I hope. 14. not exactly to me (me) not to me (me). 15. I want to speak to your aunt. 16. I will not disturb you; I won't be in your way, uncle.

Sechster Auftritt.

Frau von Dorsigny. Franz von Dorsigny.

Fr. v. Dorsigny. Nun, lieber Mann! diese Heirat —

Dorsigny. Aus dieser Heirat wird — nichts[1].

Fr. v. Dorsigny. Wie? haben wir nicht das Wort des Vaters?

Dorsigny. Freilich wohl[2]! Aber der Sohn kann unsere Tochter nicht heiraten.

Fr. v. Dorsigny. So? und warum [denn] nicht?

Dorsigny (mit starkem Tone)[3]. Weil — weil er — tot ist.

Fr. v. Dorsigny. Mein Gott, welcher Zufall[4]!

- **Dorsigny.** Es ist ein rechter Jammer[5]. Dieser junge Mann war, was die[6] meisten jungen Leute sind, so ein kleiner Wüstling[7]. Einen Abend bei einem Balle fiel's ihm ein[8], einem artigen hübschen Mädchen den Hof zu machen[9]; ein Nebenbuhler mischte sich drein[10] und erlaubte sich beleidigende Scherze[11]. Der junge Lormeuil, lebhaft[12], aufbrausend[13], wie man es mit 20 Jahren ist[14], nahm das übel; zum Unglück[15] war er an einen Raufer von Profession geraten[16], der sich nie schlägt, ohne seinen Mann — zu töten. Und diese böse Gewohnheit behielt auch jetzt die Oberhand über die Geschicklichkeit seines Gegners[17]: der

---

1. this marriage will come to nothing (nought). 2. to be sure, we have. 3. emphatically; in a firm tone of voice 4. what an unfortunate accident. 5. a dreadful misfortune. 6. as. 7. a little bit of a rake. 8. one night at a ball he took it into his head. 9. to show great attentions to; to be ostentatiously polite to; (*slang*: to be very sweet on . . .'. 10. tried to interfere; interfered. 11. and presumed to indulge in offensive jokes (chaff). 12. passionate; easily roused. 13. hot (quick) tempered; hotspurred. 14. as one is apt to be (as one usually is) at twenty. 15. unfortunately. 16. he had come across a professed duellist (bully). 17. got also this time the better of his adversary's skill.

Sohn meines armen Freundes blieb auf dem Platze[1], mit
drei töblichen — Stichen im Leibe.

Fr. v. Dorsigny. Barmherziger Himmel! Was muß
der Vater dabei gelitten haben[2]!

Dorsigny. Das können Sie denken[3]! Und die[4]
Mutter.

Fr. v. Dorsigny. Wie? Die[4] Mutter! Die ist
ja im letzten Winter gestorben[5], soviel[6] ich weiß.

Dorsigny. Diesen[7] Winter — ganz recht! Mein
armer Freund Lormeuil! Den Winter stirbt ihm seine Frau[8],
und jetzt im Sommer muß er den Sohn in einem Duell
verlieren! — Es ist mir auch schwer angekommen[9], ihn in
seinem Schmerz zu verlassen! Aber der Dienst ist jetzt so
scharf! — Auf den zwanzigsten müssen alle Offiziere —
beim Regiment sein[10]! Heute ist der neunzehnte[11], und
ich habe nur einen Sprung nach Paris gethan[12] und muß
schon heute abend[13] [wieder] — nach meiner Garnison zurückreisen.

Fr. v. Dorsigny. Wie? So bald?

Dorsigny. Das ist einmal der Dienst[14]. Was ist
zu machen[15]? Jetzt auf unsere Tochter zu kommen[16] —

Fr. v. Dorsigny. Das liebe Kind ist sehr niedergeschlagen und schwermütig, seitdem Sie weg wären.

Dorsigny. Wissen Sie, was ich denke? Diese Partie,
die wir ausgesucht[17], war — nicht nach[18] ihrem Geschmack.

Fr. v. Dorsigny. So? Wissen Sie[19]?

---

1. was left on the ground. 2. what must have been the
sufferings of his father. 3. that you may easily imagine. 4. his.
5. why, she died. 6. as far as. 7. last. 8. last winter he lost
his wife. 9. I felt very reluctant; I was very loth; it went very
near my heart. 10. by the 20th all the officers must have joined
the (their) regiment. 11. the 19th. 12. I've only just run up to Paris.
13. this very evening. 14. such is military service. 15. to be done.
16. now to speak of . . .; now about our daughter. 17. the
match we arranged for her. 18. to. 19. do you know it.

Dorſigny. Ich weiß nichts. — Aber ſie iſt fünf=
zehn Jahre alt. — Kann ſie nicht für ſich ſelbſt ſchon ge=
wählt haben[1], eh wir es für ſie thaten?

Fr. v. Dorſigny. Ach Gott ja! Das begegnet alle
Tage[2]

Dorſigny. Zwingen möcht ich ihre Neigung nicht gern[3].

Fr. v. Dorſigny. Bewahre uns Gott davor[4]!

Siebenter Auftritt.

Die Vorigen. Sophie.

Sophie (beim Anblicke Dorſignys ſtutzend). Ah! mein
Vater —

Fr. v. Dorſigny. Nun, was iſt dir[5]? Fürchteſt
du dich, deinen Vater zu umarmen?

Dorſigny (nachdem er ſie umarmt, für ſich[6].) Sie haben's
doch gar gut, dieſe Väter[7]! Alles[8] umarmt ſie!

Fr. v. Dorſigny. Du weißt wohl noch nicht[9], Sophie,
daß ein unglücklicher[10] Zufall deine Heirat getrennt hat[11]?

Sophie. Welcher Zufall?

Fr. v. Dorſigny. Herr von Cormenil iſt tot.

Sophie. Mein Gott!

Dorſigny (hat ſie mit den Augen fixiert)[12]. Ja, nun —
was ſagſt du dazu, meine Sophie[13]?

---

1. might (can) she not have chosen for herself. 2. that
happens (such things happen) every day. 3. I should not like to
force . . . 4. heaven forbid (forfend; nicht „forefend", wie es
allgemein, aber unrichtig geſchrieben wird. v. Skeat, etymol. Wörter=
buch). 5. what's the matter. 6. aside. 7. what lucky fellows
these fathers are („dogs" anſtatt „fellows" *slang*, aber nicht
ſelten im Munde eines jungen Offiziers, der „für ſich" ſpricht).
8. every body. 9. you do not yet know (you have not yet heard),
I suppose. 10. sad. 11. to put an end to . . . 12. looking at
her steadfastly (firmly); watching her closely. 13. my dear; my
darling.

Sophie. Ich, mein Vater? — Ich beklage diesen unglücklichen Mann[1] von Herzen — aber ich kann es nicht anders als für ein Glück ansehen[2], daß — daß sich der Tag verzögert[3], der mich von Ihnen trennt.

Dorsigny. Aber, liebes Kind! wenn du gegen diese Heirat — etwas einzuwenden hattest[4], warum sagtest du uns nichts davon[5]? Wir denken ja nicht daran[6], deine Neigung zwingen zu wollen[7].

Sophie. Das weiß ich, lieber Vater — aber die[8] Schüchternheit —

Dorsigny. Weg mit der[9] Schüchternheit! Rede offen! Entdecke mir dein Herz.

Fr. v. Dorsigny. Ja, mein Kind! Höre deinen Vater! Er meint es gut, er wird dir gewiß das Beste[10] raten.

Dorsigny. Du haßtest also diesen Lormeuil zum voraus — recht herzlich?

Sophie. Das nicht[11], aber ich liebte ihn nicht.

Dorsigny. Und du möchtest keinen heiraten, als den du wirklich liebst[12]?

Sophie. Das ist wohl[13] natürlich.

Dorsigny. Du liebst also[14] — einen andern?

Sophie. Das habe ich nicht gesagt[15].

Dorsigny. Nun, nun, beinahe doch[16]. — Heraus mit der Sprache[17]! Laß mich alles wissen.

---

1. gentleman. 2. however, I can't help looking upon it as a piece of good luck. 3. is put off (postponed). 4. if you had some objection to . . .; if you objected to . . . 5. why didn't you say so. 6. we haven't the slightest intention; we don't in the least want; we don't at all desire 7. to force. 8. my. 9. your. 10. for the best. 11. not exactly. 12. and you would not like to marry any one you do not really love. 13. perfectly; quite. 14. then you do love . . . 15. I didn't say so; I've not said so. 16. very nearly; almost, if not quite. 17. speak quite plainly, please, do.

Fr. v. Dorsigny. Fasse Mut, mein Kind! Vergiß, daß es dein Vater ist, mit dem du redest.

Dorsigny. Bilde dir ein, daß du mit deinem besten, deinem zärtlichsten[1] Freunde sprächest[2] — und der, den du liebst, weiß er, daß er — geliebt wird.

Sophie. Behüte der Himmel! Nein.

Dorsigny. Ist's noch ein junger Mensch?

Sophie. Ein sehr liebenswürdiger junger Mann, und der mir darum doppelt wert ist[3], weil jedermann findet, daß er Ihnen gleicht — ein Verwandter von uns[4], der unsern Namen führt[5]. — Ach! Sie müssen ihn erraten[6].

Dorsigny. Noch nicht ganz, liebes Kind!

Fr. v. Dorsigny. Aber ich errat' ihn! Ich wette, es ist Ihr Vetter, Franz Dorsigny.

Dorsigny. Nun Sophie, du antwortest nichts?

Sophie. Billigen Sie meine Wahl?

Dorsigny (seine Freude unterdrückend, für sich). Wir müssen den Vater spielen. — Aber, mein Kind — das müssen wir [denn] doch bedenken[7].

Sophie. Warum bedenken[8]? Mein Vetter ist der beste, verständigste —

Dorsigny. Der[9]? Ein Schwindelkopf ist er, ein Wildfang[10], der in[11] den zwei Jahren, daß er weg ist[12], nicht zweimal an seinen Onkel geschrieben hat.

Sophie. Aber mir hat er desto fleißiger[13] geschrieben, mein Vater!

---

1. your most beloved; your dearest . . . 2. think you were (are) speaking to . . . 3. and whom I like so much the more. 4. of ours. 5. to bear. 6. to guess who it is; to guess his name. 7. that has to be well considered; that must be taken into the most careful consideration. 8. why should it. 9. he. 10. he is a thoughtless fellow and a regular mad cap; he is a harebrained, wild sort of a fellow. 11. during. 12. that he has been away. 13. the more frequently (regularly).

2*

Dorſigny. So? hat er das[1]? Und du haſt ihm wohl — friſchweg[2] geantwortet? Haſt du? Nicht[3]?

Sophie. Nein, ob ich gleich große Luſt dazu hatte[4]. — Nun, Sie verſprachen mir ja dieſen Augenblick[5], daß Sie meiner Neigung nicht entgegen ſein wollten[6]. — Liebe Mutter, reden[7] Sie doch für mich!

Fr. v. Dorſigny. Nun, nun, gib nach, lieber Dor= ſigny. — Es iſt da weiter nichts zu machen[8] — und geſteh nur, ſie hätte nicht beſſer wählen können[9].

Dorſigny. Es iſt wahr, es läßt ſich manches dafür ſagen[10]. — Das Vermögen iſt von[11] beiden Seiten gleich, und geſetzt[12], der[13] Vetter hätte auch ein bißchen leichtſinnig gewirtſchaftet[14], ſo weiß man[15] ja, die Heirat bringt einen jungen Menſchen — ſchon in Ordnung[16]. — Wenn ſie ihn [nun] überdies[17] lieb hat —

Sophie. O recht ſehr, lieber Vater! — Erſt in dem Augenblicke, da man mir den Herrn von Lormeuil zum Ge= mahl vorſchlug, merkte ich[18], daß ich dem Vetter gut ſei[19], — ſo was man gut ſein nennt[20]. — Und wenn mir der Vetter nun [auch] wieder gut wäre[21] —

Dorſigny (feurig). Und warum ſollte er das nicht,

---

1. indeed! he has, has he; ah! did he though. 2. straigth-way; without much ado. 3. haven't you. 4. though I should have very much liked to do so; though I had a great desire (mind, wish) to do so. 5. just now. 6. that you did not wish to op-pose . . . 7. to intercede for. 8. there is nothing else to be done. 9. she couldn't have chosen better (made a better choice). 10. there is much (a good deal) to be said in favour of it. 11. on. 12. and even supposing. 13. her. 14. had been rather extra-vagant in his expenses; had been going it rather fast. 15. every-body. 16. soon brings a young man (youngster) to his senses. 17. in addition; into the bargain; besides. 18. not till I was told that Mr. L. was to be my future husband did I feel (find out). 19. that I was very fond of (liked). 20. what is called being fond of (liking). 21. and if . . . were to love me in return.

meine Teuerste[1] — (sich besinnend)[2] meine gute Tochter! —
Nun wohl! Ich bin ein guter Vater und ergebe mich!

Sophie. Ich darf also jetzt an den Vetter schreiben?

Dorsigny. Was du willst[3]. — (Für sich). Wie hübsch
spielt sich's den Vater[4], wenn man so allerliebste Geständ=
nisse zu hören bekommt[5]!

Achter Auftritt.

Vorige. Frau von Mirville. Champagne als
Postillon mit der Peitsche klatschend.

Champagne. He, Holla!

Fr. v. Mirville. Platz[6]! da kommt ein Kurier.

Fr. v. Dorsigny. Es ist Champagne.

Sophie. Meines Vetters Bedienter!

Champagne. Gnädiger Herr — gnädige Frau[7]!
Reißen Sie mich aus[8] meiner Unruhe! — Das Fräulein
ist doch nicht schon Frau von Lormeuil[9]?

Fr. v. Dorsigny. Nein, guter Freund, noch nicht.

Champagne. Noch nicht? Dem Himmel sei Dank[10],
ich bin doch noch zeitig genug[11] gekommen, meinem armen
Herrn das Leben zu retten.

Sophie. Wie? dem Vetter ist doch kein Unglück
begegnet?

Fr. v. Dorsigny. Mein Neffe ist doch nicht krank?

Fr. v. Mirville. Du machst mir Angst[12], was ist
meinem Bruder[13]?

Champagne. Beruhigen Sie sich, gnädige Frau!

---

1. and why shouldn't he, dearest. 2. correcting himself (re-
collecting himself). 3. whatever you please. 4. how delightful
(jolly) it is to play the part of a father. 5. to get to hear. 6. make
room. 7. honoured sir (your honour), honoured madam (your
honour). 8. to relieve from. 9. Madame de L. 10. heaven be praised.
11. in time; early enough; not too late. 12. you frighten me.
13. what has happened (has anything happened) to my brother.

Mein Herr befindet sich ganz wohl, aber wir sind in einer grausamen Lage[1]. — Wenn Sie wüßten — doch Sie werden alles erfahren[2]. Mein Herr hat sich zusammengenommen[3], der gnädigen Frau, die er seine gute Tannte nennt, sein Herz auszuschütten; Ihnen verdankt er alles, was[4] er ist; zu[5] Ihnen hat er das größte Vertrauen. — Hier schreibt er Ihnen, lesen Sie[6] und beklagen Sie ihn!

Dorsigny. Mein Gott, was ist das[7]?

Fr. v. Dorsigny (liest).[8] „Beste Tante! Ich erfahre soeben[9], daß Sie im Begriffe sind, meine Cousine zu verheiraten[10]. Es ist nicht mehr Zeit, zurückzuhalten[11]: ich liebe Sophien. — Ich flehe Sie an, beste Tante, wenn sie nicht eine heftige Neigung zu ihrem bestimmten Bräutigam hat[12], [so] schenken Sie sie mir! Ich liebe sie so innig, daß ich gewiß noch[13] ihre Liebe gewinne. Ich folge dem Champagne auf dem Fuße nach[14]; er wird Ihnen diesen Brief überbringen, Ihnen erzählen, was ich seit jener[15] schrecklichen Nachricht ausgestanden habe."

Sophie. Der gute Vetter!

Fr. v. Mirville. Armer Dorsigny!

Champagne. Nein, es läßt sich gar nicht beschreiben[16], was mein armer Herr gelitten hat! Aber, lieber Herr, sagte ich zu ihm, vielleicht ist noch nicht alles ver-

---

1. dreadful fix. 2. but you shall learn all. 3. has made up his mind. 4. he has to thank you for all that ... 5. in. 6. read it (please). 7. what's the matter. 8. reading. 9. I've just learnt (learned). 10. that you are about to dispose of my cousin in marriage; that you are on the point of marrying my cousin to a stranger. 11. it is no longer proper to keep silent; there's no longer any time to lose; it's high time now to speak. 12. if she do not feel a strong attachment (a warm affection) for her intended husband (bridegroom). 13. that I am sure to ... 14. I follow close upon (I am close at) the heels of ... 15. since I'm in possession of that ... 16. it's utterly impossible to describe (to give you an idea of) ...

loren. — Geh, Schurke, sagte er zu mir, ich schneibe dir die Kehle ab, wenn du zu spät kommst. — Er kann zuweilen derb sein, Ihr lieber Neffe.

Dorsigny. Unverschämter!

Champagne. Nun, nun, Sie werden ja ordentlich[1] böse, als wenn ich von Ihnen spräche; was ich sage, geschieht aus lauter Freundschaft für ihn[2], damit Sie ihn bessern, weil Sie sein Onkel sind.

Fr. v. Mirville. Der gute, redliche Diener! Er will nichts als das Beste[3] seines Herrn!

Fr. v. Dorsigny. Geh, guter Freund, ruhe dich aus[4]! Du wirst es nötig haben[5].

Champagne. Ja, Ihr Gnaden[6], ich will mich ausruhen in der Küche. (ab.)

Neunter Auftritt.
Vorige ohne Champagne.

Dorsigny. Nun, Sophie! was sagst du dazu?

Sophie. Ich erwarte Ihre Befehle, mein[7] Vater!

Fr. v. Dorsigny. Es ist [da] weiter nichts zu thun[8]; wir müssen sie ihm ohne Zeitverlust zur Frau geben[9].

Fr. v. Mirville. Aber der Vetter ist ja noch nicht hier.

Fr. v. Dorsigny, Seinem Briefe nach[10] kann er nicht lang ausbleiben[11].

Dorsigny. Nun — wenn es denn nicht anders

---

1. well, you are getting quite . . . 2. all I do say, I say from (out of) pure friendship for him. 3. all he does is for the good (benefit) of . . . 4. rest yourself; take some rest. 5. you must want (require) it. 6. your honour. 7. I await your pleasure, my dear . . .; I await your commands . . . 8. there's no alternative left us. 9. we must let him marry her; we must give her to him in marriage; we must arrange the wedding. 10. according to . . . 11. he can't (won't) be long in coming; he'll be here in a very short time.

ist[1] — und wenn Sie so meinen[2], meine Liebe — so sei's![3]
Ich bin's zufrieden und will mich so einrichten[4], daß der
Lärm[5] der Hochzeit — vorbei ist, wenn ich zurückkomme.
— Heda[6]! Bediente!

Zehnter Auftritt.

Zwei Bediente treten ein und warten im Hintergrund[7]. **Vorige.**

Fr. v. Dorsigny. Noch eins[8]! Ihr Pachter hat
mir während Ihrer Abwesenheit zweitausend Thaler in
Wechseln ausbezahlt — ich habe ihm eine Quittung darüber
gegeben. — Es ist Ihnen doch recht[9]?

Dorsigny. Mir ist alles recht, was Sie thun[10], meine
Liebe! (Während sie die Wechsel aus einer Schreibtafel hervorholt, zu
Frau von Mirville.) Darf ich[11] das Geld wohl nehmen?

Fr. v. Mirville. Nimm es ja, sonst machst du dich
verdächtig.

Dorsigny (heimlich zu ihr)[12]. In Gottes Namen[13]!
Ich will meine Schulden damit bezahlen! (Laut, indem er die
Wechsel der Frau von Dorsigny in Empfang nimmt[14].) Das Geld er-
innert mich, daß ein verwünschter Schelm von[15] Wucherer
mich schon seit lange[16] um hundert Pistolen plagt[17], die
— mein Neffe von ihm geborgt hat. — Wie ist's[18]? Soll
ich den Posten bezahlen?

Fr. v. Mirville. Ei, das versteht sich[19]! Sie wer=

---

1. if it must be. 2. and you think so. 3. then let it be so.
4. and I'll arrange matters so . . .; and I'll make such arrange-
ments . . . 5. noise; trouble; bother; bustle. 5. holla there.
7. at the back of the stage. 8. one thing more. 9. it's all right,
I suppose. 10. certainly, I sanction (approve of, agree to) all you
do. 11. shall I; may I; ought I to. 12. aside to her. 13. very
well; all right. 14. taking the money (the notes) which Mrs D.
offers him. 15. of a. 16. for some time. 17. has been dunning
me (bothering me) for a hundred pistoles. 18. what do you think
(say). 19. of course.

ben doch meine Base keinem Bruder Liederlich zur Frau geben wollen, der bis an die Ohren in Schulden steckt[1]?

Fr. v. Dorsigny. Meine Nichte hat recht[2], und was übrigbleibt[3], kann man zu Hochzeitgeschenken anwenden[4].

Fr. v. Mirville. Ja, ja, zu Hochzeitgeschenken!

Ein dritter Bedienter (kommt). Die Modehändlerin der Frau von Mirville.

Fr. v. Mirville. Sie kommt wie gerufen[5]. Ich will gleich den Brautanzug bei[6] ihr bestellen. (ab).

Elfter Auftritt.
Vorige ohne Frau v. Mirville.

Dorsigny (zu den Bedienten). Kommt her! (Zur Frau von Dorsigny). Man wird nach dem Herrn Gaspar, unserm Notar, schicken müssen[7]. —

Fr. v. Dorsigny. Lassen Sie ihn lieber gleich zum Nachtessen einladen[8]; dann können wir alles nach Bequemlichkeit[9] abmachen.

Dorsigny. Das ist wahr! (Zu einem von den Bedienten.) Du, geh zum Juwelier und laß ihn das Neueste herbringen, was er hat[10]. — (Zu einem andern.) Du gehst zum Herrn Gaspar, unserm Notar, ich lass' ihn bitten[11], heute mit mir zu Nacht zu essen[12]. — Dann bestellest du vier Postpferde; Punkt elf Uhr müssen sie vor dem Hause sein[13], denn ich muß in der Nacht noch fort[14]. — (Zu einem dritten) Für

---

1. I hope you won't marry my cousin to a scapegrace (to a bit of a rake) who is head over ears (up to his ears) in debt. 2. is right. 3. the remainder (the rest). 4. can be spent in . . . 5. in the very nick of time. 6. from. 7. we must send for. 8. you had better ask him at once to supper. 9. everything comfortably. 10. tell him to bring the newest things he has. 11. and say I beg (ask) him . . . 12. to sup (to take supper) with me to-night. 13. they must be here punctually at eleven o'clock (at 11 sharp). 14. for I must be off this very night.

dich, Jasmin, hab' ich einen kitzlichen Auftrag — du hast
Kopf[1]; dir kann man was anvertrauen[2].

Jasmin. Gnädiger Herr, das beliebt Ihnen so zu sagen[3].

Dorsigny. Du weißt, wo Herr Simon wohnt, der
Geldmäkler, der sonst meine Geschäfte machte[4] — der mei=
nem Neffen immer mein eignes Geld borgte[5].

Jasmin. Ei jawohl[6]! Warum sollt' ihn nicht
kennen! Ich war ja immer der Postillon des gnädigen
Herrn, Ihres[7] Neffen.

Dorsigny. Geh zu ihm, bring[8] ihm diese hundert
Pistolen, die mein Neffe ihm schuldig ist, und die ich ihm
hiermit bezahle! Vergiß aber nicht, dir einen Empfang=
schein geben zu lassen[9].

Jasmin. Warum nicht gar[10]. — Ich werde doch
kein solcher Esel sein! (Die Bedienten gehen ab.)

Fr. v. Dorsigny. Wie er sich verwundern wird,
der gute Junge[11]; wenn er morgen ankommt und die Hoch=
zeitgeschenke eingekauft, die Schulden bezahlt findet[12].

Dorsigny. Das glaub' ich[13]! Es thut mir nur
leid, daß ich nicht Zeuge davon sein kann!

Zwölfter Auftritt.
Vorige. Frau von Mirville.

Fr. v. Mirville (eilt herein, heimlich zu ihrem Bruder[14]).
Mach', daß du fortkommst[15], Bruder! Eben kommt der

---

1 you're a 'cute (acute) fellow. 2. one can entrust a delicate
commission to you (trust you with). 3. it pleases you to say so (you
are pleased to say so). 4. who formerly managed my affairs. 5. who
always lent ... to my ... 6. certainly, I do. 7. the messenger of his
honour, your ... 8. go and bring him. 9. to ask for; to make him
give you. 10. o dear no, sir; certainly not sir. 11. the good youngster, won't he look surprised. 12. and finds the wedding-presents
bought, and his debts paid. 13. that I do believe; I can well believe
that; I believe you. 14. entering hastily and speaking to her brother
in a low voice. 15. off with you directly; take yourself off at once.

Onkel[1] mit einem Herrn an, der mir ganz so aussieht, wie[2] der Herr von Lormeuil.

Dorsigny (in ein Kabinett fliehend)[3]. Das wäre der Teufel[4].

Fr. v. Dorsigny. Nun, warum eilen Sie denn so schnell fort, Dorsigny?

Dorsigny. Ich muß — ich habe — gleich werd' ich wieder da sein[5].

Fr. v. Mirville (pressiert). Kommen Sie, Tante! Sehen Sie doch die schönen Mützen an[6], die man[7] mir ge= bracht hat.

Fr. v. Dorsigny. Du thust recht, mich zu Rat zu ziehen[8]. Ich verstehe mich darauf[9]. Ich will dir aus= suchen helfen.

Dreizehnter Auftritt.

Oberst Dorsigny. Lormeuil. Frau v. Dorsigny. Sophie. Frau von Mirville.

Oberst. Ich komme früher zurück[10], Madame, als ich gedacht habe, aber desto besser! — Erlauben Sie, daß ich Ihnen hier[11] diesen Herrn —

Fr. v. Dorsigny. Bitte tausendmal um Vergebung, meine Herren[12] — die Putzhändlerin wartet auf uns, wir sind gleich wieder da[13]. — Komm, meine Tochter!

Oberst. Nun, nun, diese Putzhändlerin könnte wohl auch einen Augenblick warten, dächt' ich[14].

---

1. uncle has just arrived. 2. who looks uncommonly like ... 3. hurrying. 4. confound it all; the deuce, he does. 5. I shall be back again directly. 6. do, please, my dear aunt, come and look at ... 7. they. 8. to ask my ... 9. I understand these things. 10. I've come back (returned) earlier. 11. allow (permit) me to introduce ... 12. I beg (ask) a thousand pardons, gent- lemen. 13. cf Anm. 5. 14. I should think.

Sophie. Eben darum, weil sie[1] nicht warten kann — entschuldigen Sie, meine Herren[2]. (ab.)

Oberst. Das mag sein[3] — aber ich sollte doch denken[4] —

Fr. v. Mirville. Die Herren, wissen wir wohl, fragen nach Putzhändlerinnen nichts[5]; aber für uns sind das sehr wichtige Personen[6]. (Geht ab, sich tief gegen Lormeuil verneigend.)

Oberst. Zum Teufel[7], das seh' ich, daß man uns ihretwegen stehen läßt[8].

Vierzehnter Auftritt.
Oberst Dorsigny. Lormeuil.

Oberst. Ein schöner Empfang[9], [das] muß ich sagen!

Lormeuil. Ist das so der Brauch bei[10] den Pariser Damen[11], daß[12] sie den Putzhändlerinnen nachlaufen, wenn ihre Männer ankommen?

Oberst. Ich weiß gar nicht, was ich daraus machen soll[13]. Ich schrieb, daß ich erst in sechs Wochen zurück sein könnte[14]; ich bin unversehens da[15], und man ist nicht im geringsten mehr darüber erstaunt, als wenn ich nie aus der Stadt gekommen wäre[16].

Lormeuil. Wer sind die beiden jungen Damen, die mich so höflich grüßten[17]?

---

1. it's just because she ... 2. excuse us, gentlemen. 3. may be. 4. but I really think; but I should have thought. 5. gentlemen, we know well, consider milliners to be persons of no account. 6. to us they are very important. 7. botheration. 8. that one prefers their company (society) to ours; that one neglects us for them; that we don't count for as much as they do. 9. a nice welcome. 10. with. 11. Paris ladies. 12. to (c. Inf.) 13. what to make of it; what to say to it. 14. I could not be back (return) in less than ... 15. now I arrive ... 16. than if I had never left the place (gone away). 17. who bowed to me so courteously.

Oberſt. Die eine[1] iſt meine Nichte und die andere meine Tochter, Ihre beſtimmte[2] Braut.

Cormeuil. Sie ſind beide ſehr hübſch.

Oberſt. Der Henker auch[3]! Die Frauen ſind alle hübſch in meiner Familie. Aber es iſt nicht genug an dem Hübſchſein — man muß ſich auch artig betragen[4].

Fünfzehnter Auftritt.

Vorige. Die drei Bedienten, die nach und nach[5] hereinkommen.

Zweiter Bedienter (zur Linken des Oberſten). Der Notar läßt ſehr bedauern[6], daß er mit Euer Gnaden nicht zu Nacht ſpeiſen kann — er wird ſich aber nach Tiſch einfinden[7].

Oberſt. Was ſchwatzt der da für närriſches Zeug[8].

Zweiter Bedienter. Die Poſtpferde werden Schlag elf Uhr vor[9] dem Hauſe ſein.   (ab)

Oberſt. Die Poſtpferde, jetzt, da ich eben ankomme[10]!

Erſter Bedienter (zu ſeiner rechten Seite). Der Ju= welier, Euer Gnaden, hat Bankerott gemacht[11] und iſt dieſe Nacht[12] auf und davon gegangen[13].   (ab.)

Oberſt. Was geht das mich an[14]? Er war mir nichts ſchuldig[15]!

Jasmin (an ſeiner linken Seite). Ich war bei dem[16] Herrn

---

1. one. 2. intended; promised. 3. naturally (of course) they are. 4. but simply (merely) to be pretty, won't do, one must also behave handsomely (handsome is that handsome does engliſches Sprichwort). 5. one after the other. 6. is very sorry; regrets very much. 7. call after supper; present himself afterwards. 8. what nonsense (rubbish) does that fellow talk there. 9. at. 10. now that I've just arrived. 11. has become bankrupt. 12. this night (last night). 13. has decamped (run away), (*slang*: he has cut and run; he has cut his stick; he has made tracks). 14. what's that to me; what do I care. 15. he did not owe me anything. 16. I've been to; I called on; I went to.

Simon, wie Euer Gnaden befohlen. Er war krank und lag im[1] Bette. Hier schickt er Ihnen die Quittung.

Oberst. Was für eine Quittung, Schurke?

Jasmin. Nun ja[2], die Quittung, die Sie in der[3] Hand haben. Belieben Sie zu lesen[4].

Oberst (liest). „Ich Endesunterzeichneter bekenne[5], von dem Herrn Oberst von Dorsigny zweitausend Livres, welche ich seinem Herrn Neffen vorgeschossen, [richtig] er= halten zu haben[6]“.

Jasmin. Euer Gnaden sehen, daß die Quittung richtig[7] ist.

Oberst. O vollkommen richtig! Das begreife, wer's kann: mein Verstand steht still[8]. — Der ärgste Gauner in ganz[9] Paris ist krank und schickt mir die Quittung über das, was[10] mein Neffe ihm schuldig ist.

Lormeuil. Vielleicht schlägt ihm das Gewissen[11].

Oberst. Kommen Sie! Kommen Sie, Lormeuil! Suchen wir herauszubringen[12], was uns diesen angenehmen Empfang verschafft — und hole der Teufel[13] alle Notare, Juweliere, Postpferde, Geldmäkler und Putzmacherinnen!

(Beide ab.)

———

1. in. 2. why, sir; well. 3. your. 4. be pleased to read it. 5. I, the undersigned, do hereby acknowledge. 6. the receipt of two thousand francs, duly paid to me by order of Colonel D., which I had lent to his nephew. 7. in proper order; all right; perfectly correct. 8. let him that can comprehend it all; my wit is at an end (I am at the end of my wits). 9. all. 10. for what . . . 11. perhaps his conscience smites him. 12. let us try to find out. 13. and may all the notaries . . . go to Jericko.

Zweiter Aufzug.

Erster Auftritt.

Frau von Mirville. Franz Dorsigny kommt aus einem Zimmer linker Hand[1] und sieht sich sorgfältig um.

Fr. v. Mirville (von der entgegengesetzten Seite). Wie unbesonnen! Der Onkel wird den Augenblick[2] da sein.

Dorsigny. Aber sage mir doch, was mit mir werden soll[3]? Ist alles entdeckt, und weiß meine Tante, daß ihr vorgeblicher Mann nur ihr Neffe war?

Fr. v. Mirville. Nichts weiß man! Nichts ist entdeckt[4]! Die Tante ist noch mit der Modehändlerin eingeschlossen; der Onkel flucht auf seine Frau[5] — Herr von Lormeuil ist ganz verblüfft[6] über die sonderbare Aufnahme, und ich will suchen, die Entwicklung, die nicht mehr lange anstehen kann, so lange als möglich zu verzögern[7], daß ich[8] Zeit gewinne, den Onkel zu deinem Vorteil zu stimmen[9], oder, wenn's nicht anders ist[10], den Lormeuil in mich verliebt zu machen[11] — denn eh ich zugebe, daß er die Cousine heiratet[12], nehm' ich ihn lieber selbst[13].

---

1. on the left. 2. directly. 3. what shall (is to) become of me. 4. nothing is known, nothing discovered. 5. vents his ill humour (rage) by indulging in strong (bad) language about his wife (to curse, to swear at ist hier nicht anwendbar, da der Gegenstand des Zornes abwesend ist). 6. quite taken aback by (astonished, dumbfounded at; *slang*: flabbergasted at). 7. to stave off (to delay) as long as possible the catastrophe which can't be deferred much longer. 8. in order to . . .; that I may . . . 9. to bring uncle round in your favour (to your interest). 10. if nothing else can be done; if the worst comes to the worst; if it needs must be. 11. to make L. fall in love with me. 12. sooner than let him marry our . . . 13. I would take him myself.

Zweiter Auftritt.

Vorige. Valcour.

Valcour (kommt schnell). Ah schön, schön[1], daß ich dich hier finde, Dorsigny. Ich habe dir tausend Sachen zu sagen und in der größten Eile.

Dorsigny. Hol' ihn der Teufel[2]! Der kommt mir jetzt gelegen[3].

Valcour. Die gnädige Frau darf doch[4] —

Dorsigny. Vor[5] meiner Schwester hab' ich kein Geheimniß.

Valcour (zur Frau von Mirville sich wendend). Wie freue ich mich, meine Gnädige, Ihre Bekanntschaft gerade in diesem Augenblicke zu machen, wo ich so glücklich war[6], Ihrem Herrn Bruder einen wesentlichen Dienst zu erzeigen!

Dorsigny. Was hör' ich? Seine Stimme! (Flieht in das Kabinett, wo er herausgekommen.)

Valcour (ohne Dorsignys Flucht zu bemerken, fährt fort). Sollte ich jemals in den Fall kommen, meine Gnädige, Ihnen nützlich sein zu können[7], so betrachten Sie mich als Ihren ergebensten Diener. (Er bemerkt nicht, daß indes der Oberst Dorsigny hereingekommen und sich an den Platz des andern gestellt hat[8].)

Dritter Auftritt.

Vorige. Oberst Dorsigny. Cormeuil.

Oberst. Ja — diese Weiber sind eine wahre[9] Geduldprobe für ihre Männer.

---

1. ah! capital, excellent. 2. confound that fellow. 3. he does turn up at a nice time for me. 4. I may speak in presence of Madam, I suppose. 5. from. 6. when I am so much favoured by fortune as to be able to . . . 7. if I should ever happen to be able to serve your Grace (to be of use to y. G.) 8. and taken the place of. 9. really a; a regular.

Dalcour (kehrt sich um und glaubt mit dem jungen Dorsigny zu reden[1]). Ich wollte dir also sagen[2], lieber Dorsigny, daß dein Oberstlieutenant nicht tot ist.

Oberst. Mein Oberstlieutenant?

Dalcour. Mit dem du die Schlägerei gehabt hast. Er hat an meinen Freund Liancour schreiben lassen[3]; er läßt dir vollkommene Gerechtigkeit widerfahren[4] und bekennt, daß er der Angreifer gewesen sei. Die Familie hat zwar[5] schon angefangen, dich gerichtlich zu verfolgen[6], aber wir wollen alles anwenden[7], die Sache beizeiten zu unterdrücken[8]. Ich habe mich losgemacht[9], dir diese gute Nachricht zu überbringen, und muß gleich wieder zu meiner Gesellschaft[10].

Oberst. Sehr obligiert — aber —

Dalcour. Du kannst also ganz ruhig schlafen[11]. Ich[12] wache für dich. (ab.)

Vierter Auftritt.

Frau v. Mirville. Oberst Dorsigny. Cormeuil.

Oberst. Sage mir doch, was der Mensch will[13]?

Fr. v. Mirville. Der Mensch ist verrückt[14], das sehen Sie ja[15].

Oberst. Dies scheint also eine Epidemie zu sein, die alle Welt[16] ergriffen hat, seitdem ich weg bin[17]; denn das

---

1. thinks he is speaking with ... 2. well, then, I wanted to tell you. 3. he has caused a letter to be written to ... 4. he does you complete justice. 5. it is true. 6. to proceed (to take legal proceedings) against you. 7. we'll do our best; we'll try every means in our power. 8. to put a stop to it forwith (to them sc. proceedings); to nip the whole affair in the bud. 9. I've got away. 10. and must at once get back again to my company (companions, friends). 11. no fear of any kind need therefore disturb your rest. 12. I shall. 13. what the fellow means. 14. crazy; crazed; (cracked, *slang*). 15. don't you see. 16. everybody here. 17. since I went away.

ift der erfte Narr nicht, dem ich feit einer halben Stunde
hier begegne[1].

Fr. v. Mirville. Sie müffen den trockenen Empfang
meiner Tante nicht fo hoch aufnehmen[2]. Wenn von Putz=
fachen die Rede ift[3], fo darf man ihr mit nichts anderm
kommen[4].

Oberft. Nun, Gott fei Dank! da hör' ich doch endlich
[einmal] ein vernünftiges Wort! — So magft du denn[5] die
erfte fein, die ich mit dem Herrn von Lormeuil bekannt mache[6].

Lormeuil. Ich bin fehr glücklich[7], mein Fräulein,
daß ich·mich der Einwilligung Ihres Herrn Vaters erfreuen
darf[8]. — Aber diefe Einwilligung kann mir zu nichts helfen[9],
wenn nicht die Ihrige —

Oberft. Nun fängt der auch an! Hat die allgemeine
Raferei auch dich angefteckt[10], armer Freund? Dein Kom=
pliment ift ganz artig, aber bei meiner Tochter, und nicht
bei meiner Nichte hätteft du das anbringen follen[11].

Lormeuil. Vergeben Sie, gnädige Frau! Sie fagen
der Befchreibung fo vollkommen zu[12], die mir Herr von
Dorfigny von meiner Braut gemacht hat[13], daß mein Irr=
tum verzeihlich ift.

Fr. v. Mirville. Hier kommt meine Coufine, Herr
von Lormeuil! Betrachten Sie fie recht[14], und überzeugen
Sie fich mit Ihren eigenen Augen, daß fie alle die fchönen
Sachen verdient, die· Sie mir zugedacht haben.

---

1. I've seen (met) here within the last half hour. 2. you
must not (should not) take the cold reception (the cool welcome)
so much to heart. 3. when matters of dress and millinery are
under consideration (on the tapis). 4. one must not trouble her
with anything else; one must leave her quite alone. 5. then.
6. to introduce to (to whom I present Mr. Lormeuil). 7. I greatly
rejoice; I am highly pleased. 8. to possess the . . . 9. can be
of no use to me. 10. to seize; to take hold of. 11. you should
have paid it to . . . 12 you so thoroughly answer the description.
13. has given. 14. look at her closely (carefully).

Vorige. Sophie.

Sophie. Bitte tausendmal um Verzeihung[1], bester Vater, daß ich Sie vorhin habe so stehen lassen[2], die Mama rief mir, und ich mußte ihrem Befehl[3] gehorchen.

Oberst. Nun, wenn man nur seinen Fehler[4] einsieht und sich entschuldigt —

Sophie. Ach, mein Vater, wo finde ich[5] Worte, Ihnen meine Freude, meine Dankbarkeit auszudrücken, daß Sie in diese Heirat willigen[6].

Oberst. So, so! gefällt sie dir, diese Heirat?

Sophie. O gar sehr[7]!

Oberst (leise zu Lormeuil). Du siehst, wie sie dich schon liebt, ohne dich zu kennen! Das kommt von der schönen Beschreibung, die ich ihr von dir gemacht habe, eh ich abreiste[8].

Lormeuil. Ich bin Ihnen sehr verbunden.

Oberst. Ja, aber nun, mein Kind, wird es doch wohl Zeit sein[9], daß ich mich nach deiner Mutter ein wenig umsehe[10]; denn endlich werden mir doch die Putzhändlerinnen Platz machen, hoffe ich[11]. — Leiste du indes diesem Herrn Gesellschaft[12]. Er ist mein Freund, und mich soll's freuen[13], wenn er bald auch der deinige wird — verstehst du? (Zu Lormeuil.) Jetzt frisch daran — das ist der Augenblick[14]! Suche noch heute ihre Neigung zu gewinnen[15], so ist sie

---

1. I beg a thousand pardons. 2. for having left you so unceremoniously a little while ago. 3. summons. 4. when one sees one's fault. 5. how shall I find . . . 6. that you consent to . . .; for consenting to . . . 7. oh, very much indeed. 8. before I left. 9. it is time, I think. 10. to look after . . . a little. 11. for at last, I hope, the milliners will move off (sheer off, *slang*) to make room for me. 12. meanwhile bear (keep) this gentleman company. 13. I shall be glad. 14. now look sharp (alive), now is your chance. 15. affection.

morgen[1] deine Frau. — (Zu Frau von Mirville.) Kommt, Nichte! Sie mögen es miteinander allein ausmachen[2]. (ab.)

Sechster Auftritt.
Sophie. · Cormeuil.

Sophie. Sie werden also auch bei der Hochzeit sein[3]?

Cormeuil. Ja, mein Fräulein[4] — sie scheint Ihnen nicht zu mißfallen, diese Heirat?

Sophie. Sie hat den Beifall meines Vaters.

Cormeuil. Wohl! Aber was die Väter veranstalten, hat darum[5] nicht immer den Beifall der Töchter.

Sophie. O was diese Heirat betrifft[6] — die ist auch ein wenig meine Anstalt[7].

Cormeuil. Wie das[8], mein Fräulein?

Sophie. Mein Vater war so gütig, meine Neigung um Rat zu fragen[9].

Cormeuil. Sie lieben also den Mann, der Ihnen zum Gemahl bestimmt[10] ist?

Sophie. Ich verberg' es nicht.

Cormeuil. Wie? und kennen ihn nicht einmal?

Sophie. Ich bin mit ihm erzogen worden[11].

Cormeuil. Sie wären[12] mit dem jungen Cormeuil erzogen worden?

Sophie. Mit dem Herrn von Cormeun. — Nein!

Cormeuil. Das ist aber Ihr bestimmter Bräutigam.

Sophie. Ja, das war anfangs.

Cormeuil. Wie, anfangs?

---

1. and to-morrow she'll be. 2. they may settle it between themselves alone. 3. shall you be at the wedding, too. 4. Miss Dorsigny. 5. on that account; for that reason. 6. as regards. 7. it is a little (partly) of my own arranging, too. 8. how so. 9. so kind (good) as to consult. 10. who is to become your ... 11. I was brought up with him; we were brought up together. 12. were you ...

Sophie. Ich sehe, daß Sie noch nicht wissen, mein Herr —

Cormeuil. Nichts weiß ich! Nicht das Geringste weiß ich[1].

Sophie. Er ist tot.

Cormeuil. Wer ist tot?

Sophie. Der junge Herr von Cormeuil.

Cormeuil. Wirklich?

Sophie. Ganz gewiß[2].

Cormeuil. Wer hat Ihnen gesagt, daß er tot sei?

Sophie. Mein Vater!

Cormeuil. Nicht doch[3], Fräulein! Das kann ja nicht sein, das ist nicht möglich.

Sophie. Mit Ihrer Erlaubnis, es ist! Mein Vater, der von Toulon kommt[4], muß es doch besser wissen, als Sie[5]. Dieser junge Edelmann bekam auf einem Balle Händel[6], er schlug sich[7] und erhielt drei Degenstiche [durch den Leib].

Cormeuil. Das ist gefährlich.

Sophie. Jawohl, er ist auch daran[8] gestorben.

Cormeuil. Es beliebt Ihnen, mit mir zu scherzen, gnädiges Fräulein! Niemand kann Ihnen vom Herrn von Cormeuil bessere Auskunft geben, als ich!

Sophie. Als Sie! Das wäre doch lustig[9].

Cormeuil. Ja, mein Fräulein, als ich! Denn, um es auf einmal herauszusagen[10] — ich selbst bin dieser Cormeuil und bin nicht tot, soviel ich weiß.

Sophie. Sie wären[11] Herr von Cormeuil?

---

1. not the least thing do I know. 2. most certainly. 3. surely not. 4. who has just arrived from ... 5. than you, I think (I suppose). 6. had a quarrel; got himself mixed up in a quarrel. 7. he fought a duel. 8. in consequence; of (from) them (sc. sword-thrusts). 9. that would indeed be amusing. 10. to cut the matter short; to speak quite plainly. 11. you are.

Cormeuil. Nun, für wen hielten Sie mich denn sonst[1]?

Sophie. Für einen Freund meines Vaters[2], den er zu meiner Hochzeit eingeladen.

Cormeuil. Sie halten also immer noch Hochzeit[3], ob ich gleich[4] tot bin?

Sophie. Ja freilich[5]!

Cormeuil. Und mit wem denn, wenn ich fragen darf?

Sophie. Mit meinem Cousin Dorsigny.

Cormeuil. Aber Ihr Herr Vater wird doch auch ein Wort dabei mitzusprechen haben[6]?

Sophie. Das hat er, das versteht sich! Er hat ja seine Einwilligung gegeben.

Cormeuil. Wann hätt' er sie gegeben[7]?

Sophie. Eben jetzt — ein paar Augenblicke vor Ihrer Ankunft.

Cormeuil. Ich bin ja aber mit ihm zugleich[8] gekommen.

Sophie. Nicht doch, mein Herr! Mein Vater ist vor Ihnen angekommen.

Cormeuil (an den Kopf greifend)[9]. Mir schwindelt[10] — es wird mir drehend vor den Augen[11]. — Jedes Wort, das Sie sagen, setzt mich in Erstaunen — Ihre Worte in Ehren[12], mein Fräulein, aber hierunter muß ein Geheimnis stecken[13], das ich nicht[14] ergründe.

Sophie. Wie, mein Herr — sollten Sie[15] wirklich im Ernst gesprochen haben?

---

1. well, whom else did you take me for. 2. of my father's. 3. and you intend to proceed (go on) with the wedding. 4. although. 5. of course, I do. 6. will have a word to speak (to say something) on the subject, I suppose. 7. when did he give it; when did he do so. 8. at the same time with him. 9. holding his head with his hands. 10. I feel quite giddy (dizzy). 11. the whole world is going round with me. 12. with due deference to what you say. 13. there must be some mystery at the bottom of this. 14. I cannot ... 15. have you.

Cormeuil. Im vollen, höchsten Ernst[1], mein Fräu=
lein —

Sophie. Sie wären[2] wirklich der Herr von Cor=
meuil? — Mein Gott, was hab' ich da gemacht[3]. — Wie
werde ich meine Unbesonnenheit[4] —

Cormeuil. Lassen Sie sich's nicht leid sein[5], Fräu=
lein — Ihre Neigung zu Ihrem Vetter ist ein Umstand,
den[6] man lieber vor als nach der[7] Heirat erfährt.

Sophie. Aber ich[8] begreife nicht —

Cormeuil. Ich will den Herrn von Dorsigny auf=
suchen[9] — vielleicht löst er mir das Rätsel. — Wie es sich
aber auch immer lösen mag[10], Fräulein, so sollen Sie mit
mir zufrieden sein[11], hoff' ich.   (ab).

Sophie. Er scheint ein sehr artiger Mensch — und
wenn man mich nicht zwingt, ihn zu heiraten, so soll es
mich recht sehr freuen[12], daß er nicht erstochen[13] ist.

Siebenter Auftritt.

Sophie. Oberst. Frau von Dorsigny.

Fr. v. Dorsigny. Laß uns allein[14], Sophie. (Sophie
geht ab[15].) Wie, Dorsigny, Sie können mir ins Angesicht be=
haupten[16], daß Sie nicht kurz vorhin[17] mit mir gesprochen
haben? Nun wahrhaftig, welcher andere als Sie[18], als
der Herr dieses Hauses, als der Vater meiner Tochter, als

---

1. in real, perfect earnestness. 2. are. 3. what have I done.
4. how can I (shall I) [make amends for] my imprudence. 5. do
not let that trouble you (in the least); never mind that. 6. something which . . . 7. much rather before than after. 8. but I
can't . . . 9. I'll try to find; I'll go and seek . . . 10. but let
it be solved as it may; but whatever be the solution of this mystery. 11. you will be . . . 12. I shall be very glad. 13. killed
(run through with a sword). 14. leave us (alone). 15. retires.
16. you can tell me to my face. 17. a little while ago. 18. who
else but you.

mein Gemahl endlich, hätte das thun können[1], was Sie
thaten?

Oberst. Was Teufel hätte ich[2] denn gethan?

Fr. v. Dorsigny. Muß ich Sie daran erinnern?
Wie? Sie wissen nicht mehr, daß Sie erst vor kurzem[3]
mit unsrer Tochter gesprochen, daß Sie ihre Neigung zu
unserm Neffen entdeckt haben, und daß wir eins worden
sind, sie ihm zur Frau zu geben[4], sobald er wird ange=
kommen sein[5].

Oberst. Ich weiß nicht — Madame, ob das alles[6]
nur ein Traum Ihrer Einbildungskraft ist, oder ob wirklich
ein anderer in meiner Abwesenheit meinen Platz einge=
nommen hat. Ist das letztere, so war's hohe Zeit, daß ich
kam[7]. — Dieser jemand schlägt meinen Schwiegersohn tot,
verheiratet meine Tochter und sticht mich aus bei meiner
Frau[8], und meine Frau und meine Tochter lassen sich's
beide ganz vortrefflich gefallen[9].

Fr. v. Dorsigny. Welche Verstockung! — In Wahr=
heit, Herr von Dorsigny, ich weiß mich in Ihr Betragen
nicht zu finden[10].

Oberst. Ich werde nicht klug aus dem Ihrigen[11].

Achter Auftritt.
Vorige. Frau von Mirville.

Fr. v. Mirville. Dacht' ich's doch, daß ich Sie beide
würde[12] beisammen finden. — Warum gleichen doch nicht

---

1. could have done ... 2. what on earth have I ... 3. not
many minutes ago. 4. to give her to him in marriage; to let him
marry her; to marry her to him. 5. as soon as he arrives. 6. all
this. 7. if the latter, (in the latter case) it was high time for me
to come. 8. cuts me out (supplants me) in my wife's affection
(regard, love). 9. quietly agree to (acquiesce in) it; are both
perfectly content with it; don't object to it in the least; seem
both to like it uncommonly. 10. I don't know what to make of.
11. I can't understand yours. 12. I thought I should ...

alle Haushaltungen der Ihrigen? Nie Zank und Streit[1]? Immer e i n Herz und e i n e Seele! Das ist erbaulich[2]! Das ist doch ein Beispiel[3]! Die Tante ist gefällig wie ein Engel, und. der Onkel geduldig wie Hiob.

Oberst. Wahr gesprochen[4], Nichte! — Man muß Hiobs.Geduld haben wie ich, um sie bei solchem Geschwätz[5] nicht zu verlieren.

Fr. v. Dorsigny. Die Nichte hat recht, man muß so gefällig sein wie ich[6], um solche Albernheiten zu ertragen.

Oberst. Nun, Madame! Unsere Nichte hat mich seit meinem Hiersein fast nie verlassen[7]. Wollen wir sie zum Schiedsrichter[8] nehmen?

Fr. v. Dorsigny. Ich bin's vollkommen zufrieden und unterwerfe mich ihrem Ausspruch.

Fr. v. Mirville. Wovon ist die Rede[9]?

Fr. v. Dorsigny. Stelle dir vor[10], mein Mann untersteht sich, mir ins Gesicht zu behaupten, daß er's nicht gewesen sei, den[11] ich vorhin für meinen Mann hielt.

Fr. v. Mirville. Ist's möglich?

Oberst. Stelle dir vor, Nichte, meine Frau will mich glauben machen[12], daß ich hier, hier in diesem Zimmer, mit ihr gesprochen haben soll[13], in demselben Augenblicke, wo[14] ich mich auf der Touloner Poststraße schütteln ließ[15].

Fr. v. Mirville. Das ist ja ganz unbegreiflich, Onkel, — hier muß ein Mißverständnis sein[16]. — Lassen Sie mich ein paar Worte mit der Tante reden.

---

1. never any quarrel (dissension) or dispute. 2. this is comforting (quite refreshing). 3. an example for others. 4. quite true; truly said. 5. when listening to such rubbish (idle talk, senseless prattle). 6. as indulgent (kindly disposed) as I am. 7. has sarcely left me since my return. 8. as umpire (arbitress). 9. what is it all about. 10. just imagine. 11. that it was not he whom . . . 12. would (wants to) make me believe. 13. that I had spoken . . . 14. at the very moment that . . . 15. I was jolted. 16. there must be a misunderstanding somewhere.

Oberft. Sieh, wie du ihr den Kopf zurechtfeßeft[1], wenn's möglich ift; aber es wird schwer halten[2].

Fr. v. Mirville (leise zur Frau von Dorfigny). Liebe Tante, das alles ift wohl nur[3] ein Scherz von dem Onkel.

Fr. v. Dorfigny (ebenso). Freilich wohl, er müßte ja rafend fein, solches Zeug im Ernft zu behaupten[4]

Fr. v. Mirville. Wiffen Sie was? Bezahlen Sie ihn mit gleicher Münze[5] — geben Sie's ihm heim[6]! — Laffen Sie ihn fühlen, daß Sie fich nicht zum beften haben laffen[7].

Fr. v. Dorfigny. Du haft recht. Laß mich nur machen[8]!

Oberft. Wird's bald[9]? Jetzt, denk' ich, wär's genug[10].

Fr. v. Dorfigny (spottweise). Jawohl ift's genug, mein Herr — und da es die Schuldigkeit der Frau ift, nur durch[11] ihres Mannes Augen zu fehen, so erkenn' ich meinen Irrtum und will mir alles einbilden[12], was Sie wollen.

Oberft. Mit dem spöttifchen Ton kommen wir nicht weiter[13].

Fr. v. Dorfigny. Ohne Groll[14], Herr von Dor= figny! Sie haben auf[15] meine Unkoften gelacht, ich lache jetzt auf die Ihrigen, und so heben wir gegeneinander auf[16]. — Ich habe jetzt einige Befuche zu geben[17]. Wenn ich zurückkomme und Ihnen der spaßhafte Humor vergangen ift, so können wir ernfthaft miteinander reden.   (ab.)

---

1. try (endeavour) to bring her to reason. 2. that won't be an easy task. 3. all this is most likely only . . . 4. he could not assert such nonsense in real earnest, unless he were crazy (a little cracked). 5. pay him in his own coin; repay him in kind. 6. give him tit for tat; return him like for like; retaliate upon him. 7. that you won't submit being made game (a fool) of. 8. just leave it to me. 9. well, have you done. 10. it's enough now, I think. 11. with. 12. believe. 13. that ironical tone of yours won't do. 14. without any animosity; without the slightest ill feeling. 15. at. 16. and so we are quits. 17. I've now some calls to make (some visits to pay).

Oberſt (zur Frau von Mirville). Verſtehſt du ein[1] Wort von allem, was ſie da ſagt?

Fr. v. Mirville. Ich werde nicht klug daraus[2]. Aber ich will ihr folgen und der Sache auf den Grund zu kommen ſuchen[3]. (ab.)

Oberſt. Thu das, wenn du willſt. Ich geb' es rein auf[4] — ſo ganz toll und närriſch[5] hab' ich ſie noch[6] nie geſehen. Der Teufel muß in meiner Abweſenheit meine Geſtalt angenommen haben[7], um mein Haus unterſt zu oberſt zu kehren[8], anders begreif' ich's nicht.

Aeunter Auftritt.

Oberſt Dorſigny. **Champagne** ein wenig betrunken[9].

Champagne. Nun, das muß wahr ſein! — Hier lebt ſich's wie im Wirtshaus[10]. — Aber wo Teufel ſtecken ſie denn alle?[11] — Keine lebendige Seele hab' ich mehr[12] geſehen, ſeitdem ich als Kurier den Lärm angerichtet habe[13]. — Doch, ſieh da, mein gnädiger Herr[14], der Hauptmann. — Ich muß doch hören, wie unſere Sachen ſtehen. (Macht gegen den Oberſt Zeichen des Verſtändniſſes und lächelt ſelbſtgefällig.)

Oberſt. Was Teufel! Iſt das nicht der Schelm, der Champagne? — Wie kommt der hieher, und was will der Eſel[15] mit ſeinen einfältigen Grimaſſen?

Champagne (wie oben). Nun, nun, gnädiger Herr?

---

1. one. 2. I can't make it out at all. 3. and try to get at the bottom of the whole affair. 4. I give it up altogether. 5. so out-and-out silly (mad) and foolish. 6. before. 7. must have assumed my shape. 8. to turn my house topsy turvy (upside down). 9. a little tipsy (half-seas-over, *slang*). 10. one lives here as jolly as in a public house. 11. but where the dickens (deuce, devil) are they all. 12. not a living soul have I . . . 13. since I made the noise; (since I kicked up the row; *slang*, aber der Sprache des Dieners entſprechend). 14. my gracious master. 15. what does the idiot (fool, jackass) want.

Oberst. Ich glaube, der Kerl ist besoffen.

Champagne. Nun, was sagen Sie? Hab' ich meine Rolle nicht gut gespielt?

Oberst (für sich). Seine Rolle? Ich merke etwas[1] — Ja, Freund Champagne, nicht übel[2].

Champagne. Nicht übel! Was? Zum Entzücken habe ich sie gespielt. Mit meiner Peitsche und den Kurier= stiefeln, sah ich nicht einem ganzen Postillon gleich[3]? Wie?

Oberst. Ja! ja! (Für sich.) Weiß der Teufel, was ich ihm antworten soll[4].

Champagne. Nun, wie steht's drinnen[5]? Wie weit sind Sie jetzt[6]?

Oberst. Wie weit ich bin — wie's steht — nun, du kannst dir leicht vorstellen, wie's steht.

Champagne. Die Heirat ist richtig, nicht wahr[7]? — Sie haben als Vater die Einwilligung gegeben?

Oberst. Ja.

Champagne. Und morgen treten Sie in Ihrer wahren Person als Liebhaber auf.

Oberst (für sich). Es ist ein Streich von meinem Neffen[8]!

Champagne. Und heiraten die Witwe des Herrn von Lormeuil — Witwe! Hahaha! — Die Witwe von meiner Erfindung[9].

Oberst. Worüber lachst du?

Champagne. Das fragen Sie? Ich lache über die Gesichter, die der ehrliche Onkel schneiden wird, wenn er in vier Wochen zurückkommt und Sie mit[10] seiner Tochter verheiratet findet.

---

1. I begin to see; (oh, I twig, *slang*). 2. very well; not badly. 3. didn't I look quite the postilion. 4. devil a bit do I know what to answer him; I'll be hanged, if I know ... 5. how do matters stand in there; how do we get on in there. 6. how far have you got by this time. 7. is all right, isn't it (ain't it). 8. of my nephew's. 9. of my invention (making). 10. to; with.

Oberst (für ſich). Ich möchte raſend werden[1].

Champagne. Und der Bräutigam von Toulon, der mit ihm angezogen kommt[2] und einen andern[3] in ſeinem Neſte findet — das iſt himmliſch!

Oberſt. Zum Entzücken[4]!

Champagne. Und wem haben Sie alles das[5] zu danken? Ihrem treuen Champagne!

Oberſt. Dir? Wieſo?

Champagne. Nun, wer ſonſt hat Ihnen denn den Rat gegeben[6], die Perſon Ihres Onkels zu ſpielen[7]?

Oberſt (für ſich). Ha, der Schurke!

Champagne. Aber das iſt zum Erſtaunen[8], wie Sie Ihrem Onkel [doch] ſo ähnlich ſehen! Ich würde darauf ſchwören[9], er ſei es ſelbſt, wenn ich ihn nicht hundert Meilen weit von uns[10] wüßte.

Oberſt (für ſich). Mein Schelm von Neffe[11] macht einen ſchönen Gebrauch von meiner Geſtalt[12].

Champagne. Nur ein wenig zu ältlich ſehen Sie aus[13] — Ihr Onkel iſt ja ſo ziemlich von Ihren Jahren; Sie hätten nicht nötig gehabt, ſich ſo gar alt zu machen[14].

Oberſt. Meinſt du?

Champagne. Doch was thut's[15]! Iſt er doch nicht da[16], daß man eine Vergleichung anſtellen könnte. — Und

---

1. I could go mad; it's enough to drive a fellow mad.
2. who comes along with him. 3. another bird. 4. delicious; delightful. 5. for all this. 6. who else advised you. 7. to personate your . . . 8. astonishing. 9. I could have sworn. 10. from here. 11. that scamp (rascal) of a nephew of mine. 12. a nice (pretty) use of his likeness to me. 13. you look only a little bit oldish. 14. you need not have made yourself quite so old; (there was no need for you to get yourself up like an old fogey [fogie, fogy], *slang*). 15. but what does it matter; (but what's the odds, *slang*). 16. as long as he isn't here.

ein Glück für uns[1], daß der Alte[2] nicht da ist. Es würde uns schlecht bekommen[3], wenn er zurückkäme.

Oberst. Er ist zurückgekommen.

Champagne. Wie? Was?

Oberst. Er ist zurückgekommen, sag' ich.

Champagne. Um Gotteswillen[4], und Sie stehen[5] hier? Sie bleiben ruhig? Thun Sie, was Sie wollen — Helfen Sie sich, wie Sie können — ich suche das Weite[6].

(Will fort[7]).

Oberst. Bleib, Schurke! zweifacher[8] Halunke, bleib! Das also[9] sind deine schönen Erfindungen, Herr Schurke?

Champagne. Wie, gnädiger Herr, ist das mein Dank?

Oberst. Bleib, Halunke! Wahrlich, meine Frau (hier macht Champagne eine Bewegung des Schreckens[10]) ist die Närrin nicht, für die ich sie hielt[11] — und einen solchen Schelmen= streich sollte ich so hingehen lassen[12]? — Nein, Gott ver= damm' mich[13], wenn ich nicht auf der Stelle meine volle Rache dafür nehme. — Es ist noch nicht so spät. Ich eile zu meinem Notar. Ich bring' ihn mit[14]. Noch heute nacht heiratet Lormeuil meine Tochter. — Ich überrasche meinen Neffen — er muß [mir] den Heiratskontrakt seiner Base noch selbst mit unterzeichnen. — Und was dich betrifft[15], Halunke —

Champagne. Ich, gnädiger Herr, ich will mit unter=

---

1. and lucky for us. 2. that the old chap (cove, *slang*). 3. we should catch it; we should get it hot and strong. 4 for heaven's sake; good heavens. 5. stay; remain. 6. I make myself scarce; I'll cut my stick; (beides sind *slang*-Ausdrücke, aber ganz passend hier); I'll be off directly. 7. about to go. 8. double-dis- tilled; compound; out-and-out. 9. these then . . . 10. here Ch. gives a start. 11. is not the fool I took her for; is not so foolish as I thought. 12. and I should permit such a rascally trick (such knavery, roguery) to go unpunished. 13. curse me. 14. with me. 15. and as for you.

zeichnen[1] — ich will auf der Hochzeit mittanzen, wenn Sie's befehlen.

Oberst. Ja, Schurke, ich will dich tanzen machen! — Und die Quittung über die hundert Pistolen, merk' ich jetzt wohl[2], habe ich auch nicht der Ehrlichkeit des Wucherers zu verdanken. — Zu meinem Glück hat der Juwelier Bankerott gemacht. — Mein Taugenichts von Neffe begnügte sich nicht[3], seine Schulden mit meinem Gelde zu bezahlen; er macht auch noch neue auf meinen Krebit[4]. — Schon gut[5]! — Er soll mir dafür bezahlen! Und du, ehrlicher Gesell, rechne auf eine tüchtige Belohnung. — Es thut mir leid, daß ich meinen Stock nicht bei[6] mir habe; aber aufgeschoben ist nicht aufgehoben[7]. (ab.)

Champagne. Ich falle aus den Wolken[8]! Muß dieser verwünschte Onkel auch gerade jetzt zurückkommen und mir in den Weg laufen[9], recht ausdrücklich, um mich plaudern zu machen[10]. — Ich Esel, daß ich ihm auch erzählen mußte[11]. — Ja, wenn ich noch wenigstens ein Glas zu viel getrunken hätte[12]. — Aber so[13]!

Zehnter Auftritt.

Champagne. Franz Dorsigny. Frau v. Mirville.

Fr. v. Mirville (kommt sachte hervor[14] und spricht in die Scene zurück[15]). Das Feld ist rein[16] — du kannst herauskommen — es ist niemand hier als Champagne.

---

1. I will sign it, too; I'll sign it along with him. 2. I now see well enough. 3. is (was) not content. 4. he runs up new ones on my score (and has them put down to my account). 5. very good; all right. 6. with. 7. but forbearance is no acquittance; a day of reckoning will surely come. 8. I fall from the clouds; (I'm struck all of a heap, *slang*). 9. and cross my path (way). 10. to make me blab. 11. what an ass (a jackass) I was to tell him all; what a fool I must have been to... 12. if, at least, I had taken a drop too much. 13. but as it is. 14. appears cautiously (softly) on the stage. 15. speaking into the side-scene. 16. the coast is clear.

Dorsigny (tritt ein).

Champagne (kehrt sich um und fährt zurück[1], da er ihn erblickt[2]). Mein Gott, da kommt er schon [wieder] zurück! Jetzt wird's losgehen[3]. (Sich Dorsigny zu Füßen werfend). Barmherzigkeit, gnädiger Herr! Gnade — Gnade einem armen Schelm[4], der ja unschuldig — der es freilich verdient hätte —

Dorsigny. Was soll denn das vorstellen[5]? Steh auf! Ich will dir ja nichts zuleide thun[6].

Champagne. Sie wollen mir nichts thun, gnädiger Herr —

Dorsigny. Mein Gott, nein! Ganz im Gegenteil, ich bin recht wohl mit dir zufrieden, da du deine Rolle so gut gespielt hast[7].

Champagne (erkennt ihn). Wie, Herr, sind Sie's?

Dorsigny. Freilich bin ich's.

Champagne. Ach Gott[8]! Wissen Sie, daß Ihr Onkel hier ist?

Dorsigny. Ich weiß es. Was denn weiter[9]?

Champagne. Ich hab' ihn gesehen, gnädiger Herr. Ich hab' ihn angeredet — ich dachte, Sie wären's[10]; ich hab' ihm alles gesagt, er weiß alles.

Fr. v. Mirville. Unsinniger! was hast du gethan?

Champagne. Kann ich dafür[11]? Sie sehen, daß ich eben jetzt den Neffen für den Onkel genommen — ist's zu verwundern[12], daß ich den Onkel für den Neffen nahm?

Dorsigny. Was ist zu machen[13]?

---

1. starts back. 2. at seeing him. 3. now for the row; there it goes; now for the blessed (blooming) shindy (*slang*-Ausdrücke in guter Gesellschaft unstatthaft, aber passend im Munde eines betrunkenen Bedienten). 4. have pity on (mercy upon) a poor devil. 5. what's the meaning of all this. 6. I don't want to do you any harm. 7. for having played ... so well. 8. oh, dear me. 9. well, what of that. 10. it was you. 11. is it my fault; can I help it. 12. is it to be wondered at. 13. what's to be done now.

Fr. v. Mirville. Da ist jetzt kein anderer Rat, als[1] auf der Stelle das Haus zu verlassen.

Dorsigny. Aber wenn er meine Cousine zwingt, den Cormeuil zu heiraten —

Fr. v. Mirville. Davon wollen wir morgen reden! Jetzt fort[2], geschwind! da[3] der Weg noch frei ist. (Sie führt ihn bis an die hintere Thür[4]; eben da er hinaus will[5], tritt Cormeuil aus derselben herein ihm entgegen, der ihn zurückhält[6] und wieder vorwärts führt).

Elfter Auftritt.
Die Vorigen. Cormeuil.

Cormeuil. Sind Sie's? Ich suchte Sie eben.

Fr. v. Mirville (heimlich zu Dorsigny) Es ist der Herr von Cormeuil. Er hält dich für den Onkel. Gib ihm sobald als möglich seinen Abschied[7].

Cormeuil (zur Frau von Mirville). Sie verlassen uns, gnädige Frau?

Fr. v. Mirville. Verzeihen Sie, Herr von Cormeuil. Ich bin[8] sogleich wieder hier. (Geht ab; Champagne folgt.)

Zwölfter Auftritt.
Cormeuil. Franz Dorsigny.

Cormeuil. Sie werden sich erinnern, daß Sie mich mit Ihrer Fräulein Tochter vorhin allein gelassen haben?

Dorsigny. Ich erinnere mich's[9].

Cormeuil. Sie ist sehr liebenswürdig; ihr Besitz[10] würde mich zum glücklichsten Manne[11] machen.

---

1. the only thing to be done now is . . . 2. now, off with you. 3. while. 4. to the door at the back (of the stage). 5. just as he is going out. 6. L., entering by the same, stops him. 7. give him his congé . . . 8. I shall be. 9. yes, I do. 10. to possess her. 11. the happiest of men.

Dorſigny. Ich glaub' es.

Lormeuil. Aber ich muß Sie bitten, ihrer Neigung keinen Zwang anzuthun[1].

Dorſigny. Wie iſt das?

Lormeuil. Sie iſt das liebenswürdigſte Kind von[2] der Welt, das iſt gewiß! Aber Sie haben mir ſo oft von Ihrem Neffen Franz Dorſigny geſprochen. — Er liebt Ihre Tochter!

Dorſigny. Iſt das wahr?

Lormeuil. Wie ich Ihnen ſage[3], und er wird wie= der geliebt.

Dorſigny. Wer hat Ihnen das geſagt?

Lormeuil. Ihre Tochter ſelbſt[4].

Dorſigny. Was iſt aber da zu thun? — Was raten Sie mir, Herr von Lormeuil?

Lormeuil. Ein guter Vater zu ſein.

Dorſigny. Wie?

Lormeuil. Sie haben mir hundertmal[5] geſagt, daß Sie Ihren Neffen wie einen Sohn liebten. — Nun denn, ſo geben Sie ihm Ihre Tochter! Machen Sie Ihre beiden Kinder glücklich.

Dorſigny. Aber was ſoll denn aus Ihnen werden?

Lormeuil. Aus mir? — Man will mich nicht haben[6], das iſt freilich ein Unglück[7]! Aber beklagen kann ich mich nicht darüber, da Ihr Neffe mir zuvorgekommen iſt[8].

Dorſigny. Wie? Sie wären fähig, zu entſagen[9]?

Lormeuil. Ich halte es für meine Pflicht[10].

---

1. in no way to coerce her; to let her choose for herself with absolute freedom. 2. in. 3. it is as I tell you; quite true; perfectly true. 4. herself. 5. hundreds of times. 6. I am rejected; I'm not wanted. 7. a piece of bad luck. 8. your nephew having forestalled me (having had the start of me). 9. is it possible you could make such a sacrifice (relinquish, surrender, abandon your claim on her hand). 10. I consider it my duty; I consider myself in duty bound to do so.

Dorsigny (lebhaft)[1]. Ach, Herr von Lormeuil! Wie viel Dank bin ich Ihnen schuldig[2]!

Lormeuil. Ich verstehe Sie nicht.

Dorsigny. Nein, nein, Sie wissen nicht, welchen großen, großen Dienst Sie mir erzeigen. — Ach, meine[3] Sophie! Wir werden[4] glücklich werden!

Lormeuil. Was ist das! Wie! — Das ist Herr von Dorsigny nicht. — Wär's[5] möglich —

Dorsigny. Ich habe mich verraten.

Lormeuil. Sie sind Dorsigny, der Neffe! Ja, Sie sind's — Nun, Sie habe ich zwar nicht hier gesucht, aber ich freue mich, Sie zu sehen. — Zwar sollte ich billig auf Sie böse sein[6] wegen der drei Degenstiche, die Sie mir so großmütig in den[7] Leib geschickt haben —

Dorsigny. Herr von Lormeuil!

Lormeuil. Zum Glück sind sie nicht töblich; also mag's gut sein[8]! Ihr Herr Onkel hat mir sehr viel Gutes von Ihnen gesagt[9], Herr von Dorsigny, und weit entfernt, mit Ihnen Händel anfangen zu wollen[10], biete ich Ihnen von Herzen meine[11] Freundschaft an und bitte um die Ihrige.

Dorsigny. Herr von Lormeuil!

Lormeuil. Also zur Sache[12], Herr von Dorsigny. — Sie lieben Ihre Cousine und haben vollkommen Ursache dazu[13]. Ich verspreche Ihnen, allen meinen Einfluß bei dem Obersten anzuwenden, daß sie Ihnen zu teil wird[14].

---

1. passionately. 2. how greatly am I indebted to you. 3. my dearest. 4. we may; we shall. 5. is it. 6. I ought in justice (properly) to be angry with you. 7. my. 8. so it is all right; so let that pass. 9. has spoken to me in the highest terms about you. 10. and far from wishing to quarrel with you. 11. my sincere; hearty. 12. now to the point. 13. every reason to do so. 14. that she may become yours.

4*

— Dagegen[1] verlange ich aber, daß Sie auch Ihrerseits mir einen wichtigen Dienst erzeigen.

Dorsigny. Reden Sie! Fordern Sie! Sie haben sich ein heiliges Recht auf meine Dankbarkeit erworben.

Cormeuil. Sie haben eine Schwester, Herr von Dorsigny. Da Sie aber für niemand Augen haben, als[2] für Ihre Base, so bemerkten Sie vielleicht nicht[3], wie sehr Ihre Schwester liebenswürdig ist. — Ich aber — ich habe es recht gut bemerkt — und daß ich's kurz mache[4] — Frau von Mirville verdient die Huldigung eines jeden! Ich habe sie gesehen und ich —

Dorsigny. Sie lieben sie? Sie ist die Ihre! Zählen Sie auf mich! — Sie soll Ihnen bald gut sein, wenn sie es nicht schon jetzt ist[5] — dafür steh' ich[6]. Wie sich doch alles so glücklich fügen muß[7]! — Ich gewinne einen Freund, der mir behülflich sein will, meine Geliebte zu besitzen[8], und ich bin im stande[9], ihn wieder glücklich zu machen.

Cormeuil. Das steht zu hoffen[10]; aber so ganz ausgemacht ist es doch nicht[11]. — Hier kommt Ihre Schwester! Frisch, Herr von Dorsigny — sprechen Sie für mich! Führen Sie meine Sache! Ich will bei dem Onkel die Ihrige führen. (ab).

Dorsigny. Das ist ein herrlicher Mensch, dieser Cormeuil[12]! Welche glückliche Frau wird meine Schwester[13]!

---

1. in exchange; on the other hand. 2. however, having eyes for no one but . . . 3. you may not have (perhaps you have not) noticed. 4. to cut the matter short. 5. she shall soon love you, if she does not do so already. 6. I warrant you; I vouch for it; I promise you. 7. how nicely everything seems destined to turn out for the best. 8. to obtain. 9. I am able; I am in a position. 10. it is to be hoped so. 11. but it is not by any means a matter of course. 12. he is a regular brick, this L. is. 13. how happy my sister will be as Mrs. L.

Dreizehnter Auftritt.

Frau von Mirville. Franz Dorsigny.

Fr. v. Mirville. Nun wie steht's[1], Bruder?

Dorsigny. Du hast eine Eroberung gemacht, Schwester! Der Lormeuil ist Knall und Fall sterblich in dich verliebt worden[2]. Eben hat er mir das Geständnis gethan[3], weil er glaubte, mit dem Onkel zu reden[4]! Ich sagte ihm aber, diese Gedanken sollte er sich nur vergehen lassen[5] — du hättest das Heiraten auf immer verschworen[6]. — Ich habe recht gethan, nicht[7]?

Fr. v. Mirville. Allerdings — aber — du hättest eben nicht gebraucht, ihn auf eine so rohe Art abzuweisen[8]. Der arme Junge ist schon übel genug daran[9], daß er bei Sophien durchfällt[10].

Vierzehnter Auftritt.

Vorige. Champagne.

Champagne. Nun, gnädiger Herr! machen Sie, daß Sie fortkommen[11]. Die Tante darf Sie nicht[12] mehr hier antreffen, wenn sie zurückkommt.

Dorsigny. Nun, ich gehe! Bin ich[13] doch nun gewiß, daß mir Lormeuil die Cousine nicht wegnimmt[14]

(ab mit Frau von Mirville.)

---

1. well, how do matters (does the matter) stand. 2. has all of a sudden desperately fallen in love with you; is all of a sudden over head-and-ears in love with you. 3. to make. 4. he was speaking to … 5. to dismiss this thought (to give up this idea) at once. 6. (because) you had forsworn marriage … 7. I was right, I hope, wasn't I. 8. you need not have done it so rudely. (abweisen = to reject, wenn es die Dame selbst thut). 9. is badly off already. 10. having been refused (rejected) by Sophia. 11. be off as quick as possible. 12. must not. 13. since I am. 14. won't carry off my cousin.

Fünfzehnter Auftritt.
Champagne allein.

Da bin ich nun allein! — Freund Champagne, du bist ein Dummkopf, wenn du deine Unbesonnenheit von vorhin nicht gutmachst[1]. — Dem Onkel die ganze Karte zu verraten! Aber laß[2] sehen! Was ist da zu machen? Entweder den Onkel oder den Bräutigam müssen wir uns auf[3] die nächsten zwei Tage vom Halse schaffen[4], sonst geht's nicht[5]. — Aber wie Teufel ist das anzufangen[6]? — Wart' — laß sehen. — (Nachsinnend). Mein Herr und dieser Herr von Lormeuil sind zwar als ganz gute Freunde auseinander gegangen[7], aber es hätte doch Händel zwischen ihnen setzen können[8]! Können[9], das ist mir genug! Davon laßt uns ausgehen[10]! — Ich muß als ein guter Diener Unglück verhüten! Nichts als redliche Besorgnis für meinen Herrn. — Also gleich zur Polizei! Man nimmt seine Maßregeln[11], und ist's dann meine Schuld, wenn sie den Onkel für den Neffen nehmen? — Wer kann für die[12] Ähnlichkeit? — Das Wagestück ist groß, groß, aber ich wag's[13]. Mißlingen kann's nicht, und wenn auch[14]. — Es kann nicht mißlingen. — Im äußersten Fall bin ich gedeckt[15]! Ich habe nur meine Pflicht beobachtet! Und mag dann der Onkel gegen mich toben, soviel er will — ich verstecke mich hinter den Neffen, ich verhelf' ihm zu[16] seiner Braut, er muß erkenntlich sein — Frisch, Champagne, ans Werk. — Hier ist Ehre einzulegen[17].　　　(Geht ab).

---

1. if you don't (unless you) repair the act of indiscretion you were guilty of just now. 2. let us. 3. for. 4. we must (manage to) ged rid of. 5. else it's no-go, *slang*. 6. but how the deuce is it to be managed. 7. parted, it is true, on very good terms (as very good friends). 8. there might have been a ... 9. might have been. 10. let us start from that; let this be our starting point. 11. proper measures are taken. 12. who can help the ... 13. the venture is great, but I risk it; the danger is great, but I run it. 14. and even should it ... 15. if the worst comes (come) to the worst, I'm safely out of it. 16. I help him to get (to obtain). 17. to be gained.

Dritter Aufzug.

Erster Auftritt.

Oberst Dorsigny kommt. Gleich darauf **Cormeuil.**

Oberst. Muß der Teufel auch diesen Notar gerade heute zu einem Nachtessen führen[1]! Ich hab' ihm ein Billet dort[2] gelassen, und mein Herr Neffe hat schon vorher die Mühe auf sich genommen.

Cormeuil (kommt). Für diesmal[3] denke ich [doch] wohl[4] den Onkel vor mir zu haben, und nicht den Neffen.

Oberst. Wohl bin ich's selbst[5]! Sie dürfen nicht zweifeln[6].

Cormeuil. Ich habe Ihnen viel zu sagen, Herr von Dorsigny.

Oberst. Ich glaub' es wohl, guter Junge[7]! Du wirst rasend sein vor[8] Zorn. — Aber keine Gewaltthätigkeit, lieber Freund, ich bitte darum[9]! — Denken Sie daran[10], daß der, der Sie beleidigt hat, mein Neffe ist. — Ihr Ehrenwort verlang' ich, daß Sie es mir überlassen wollen, ihn dafür zu strafen.

Cormeuil. Aber so erlauben Sie mir —

Oberst. Nichts erlaub' ich[11]! Es wird nichts daraus[12]! So seid ihr jungen Leute[13]! Ihr wißt keine

---

1. dash it all! must this notary go to a supper-party this very night; must the devil chance to take this notary to a supper-party to-night. 2. at his house. 3. this time. 4. I really hope (think, expect). 5. to be sure (indeed), 'tis myself now. 6. and no mistake; not the least doubt about it. 7. I believe you, my young friend. 8. with. 9. I beg; if you please. 10. remember; consider; don't forget. 11. no, I allow nothing. 12. it can't be done; it shall not (shan't) come to anything. 13. that's always the case with you young folks (you youngsters).

anb'ere Art, Unrecht gutzumachen[1], als daß ihr einander die Hälse brecht[2].

Cormeuil. Das ist ja aber nicht mein Fall[3]. Hören Sie doch nur[4].

Oberst. Mein Gott! ich weiß ja[5]! Bin ich doch auch jung gewesen[6]! — Aber laß dich das alles, nicht anfechten[7], guter Junge! Du wirst doch mein Schwiegersohn[8]! Du wirst's — dabei bleibt's[9]!

Cormeuil. Ihre Güte — Ihre Freundschaft erkenn' ich mit dem größten Dank. — Aber, so wie die Sachen stehen[10]

Oberst (lauter). Nichts! Kein[11] Wort mehr!

Zweiter Auftritt.

Champagne mit zwei Unteroffizieren. Vorige.

Champagne (zu diesen). Sehen Sie's, meine Herren? Sehen Sie's? Eben wollten Sie aneinander geraten[12].

Cormeuil. Was suchen[13] diese Leute bei uns?

Erster Unteroffizier. Ihre ganz[14] gehorsamen Diener, meine Herren! Habe ich nicht die Ehre, mit Herrn von Dorsigny zu sprechen? ·

Oberst. Dorsigny heiß' ich[15].

Champagne. Und dieser hier[16] ist Herr von Cormeuil?

Cormeuil. Der bin ich, ja[17]. Aber was wollen[18] diese Herren von mir?

---

1. of repairing a wrong (an injury). 2. than breaking one another's necks. 3. the case with me. 4. listen to me, pray. 5. dear me, don't I know. 6. wasn't I once young myself. 7. but never mind all that; don't let anything of that kind trouble (disquiet) you in the least. 8. you'll be ... all the same. 9. that's settled. 10. but as matters now stand. 11. not a; not one ... 12. they were just going to come to blows. 13. to want with (from). 14. most. 15. is my name. 16. and this gentleman ... 17. yes, I am. 18. cf. Anm. 13.

Zweiter Unteroffizier. Ich werde die Ehre haben, Euer Gnaden zu begleiten.

Cormeuil. Mich zu begleiten? Wohin? Es fällt mir nicht ein, auszugehen zu wollen[1].

Erster Unteroffizier (zum Obersten). Und ich, gnädiger Herr, bin beordert, Ihnen zur[2] Eskorte zu dienen.

Oberst. Aber wohin will mich der Herr[3] eskortieren?

Erster Unteroffizier. Das will ich Ihnen sagen, gnädiger Herr. Man hat in Erfahrung gebracht[4], daß Sie auf dem Sprunge stünden[5], sich mit diesem Herrn zu schlagen, und damit nun[6] —

Oberst. Mich zu schlagen! Und weswegen denn?

Erster Unteroffizier. Weil Sie Nebenbuhler sind — weil Sie beide das Fräulein von Dorsigny lieben. Dieser Herr hier ist der Bräutigam des Fräuleins, den ihr der Vater bestimmt hat — und Sie, gnädiger Herr, sind ihr Cousin und ihr Liebhaber. — O, wir wissen alles!

Cormeuil. Sie sind im Irrtum[7], meine Herren.

Oberst. Wahrlich, Sie sind an den Unrechten gekommen[8].

Champagne (zu den Wachen[9]). Frisch zu! Lassen Sie sich nichts weismachen[10], meine Herren! (Zu Herrn von Dorsigny). Lieber, gnädiger Herr! werfen Sie endlich Ihre Maske weg! Gestehen Sie, wer Sie sind! Geben Sie ein Spiel auf, wobei[11] Sie nicht die beste Rolle spielen!

Oberst. Wie, Schurke, das ist wieder ein Streich von dir[12] —

---

1. to go out. 2. as. 3. you. 4. it has been ascertained. 5. that you were on the point of . . . 6. and in order to; and lest. 7. you are mistaken. 8. upon my word, you've come to the wrong address; you sail on the wrong tack. 9. to the sergeants. 10. don't allow yourselves to be imposed upon. 11. the game in which . . . 12. a trick of yours; one of your tricks.

Champagne. Ja, gnädiger Herr, ich hab' es so veranstaltet, ich leugn' es gar nicht — ich rühme mich dessen[1]! — Die Pflicht eines rechtschaffenen Dieners habe ich erfüllt, da ich Unglück verhütete[2].

Oberst. Sie können mir's glauben[3], meine Herren! der, den Sie suchen, bin ich nicht[4], ich bin sein Onkel.

Erster Unteroffizier. Sein Onkel? Gehen Sie doch[5]! Sie gleichen dem Herrn Onkel außerordentlich[6], sagt man, aber uns soll diese Ähnlichkeit nicht betrügen.

Oberst. Aber sehen Sie mich doch nur recht an[7]! Ich habe ja eine Perücke, und mein Neffe trägt sein eigenes Haar.

Erster Unteroffizier. Ja, ja, wir wissen recht gut, warum Sie die Tracht Ihres Herrn Onkels angenommen[8]. — Das Stückchen[9] war sinnreich; es thut uns leid, daß es nicht besser geglückt ist.

Oberst. Aber, mein Herr, [so] hören Sie doch nur an[10]

Erster Unteroffizier. Ja, wenn wir jeden anhören wollten, den wir festzunehmen beordert sind — wir würden nie von der Stelle kommen. — Belieben Sie[11] uns zu folgen, Herr von Dorsigny! Die Postchaise hält vor[12] der Thür und erwartet uns[13].

Oberst. Wie? was? die Postchaise?

Erster Unteroffizier. Ja, Herr! Sie haben Ihre

---

1. I'm proud of it; I glory in it; I'm not ashamed of it. 2. in preventing ... 3. believe me. 4. I am not the one you seek (look for). 5. get along with you; nonsense. 6. you are exceedingly like ... (you and your uncle resemble one another like two peas). 7. just look at me closely (well), if you please. 8. why you've put on your uncle's clothes; why you have assumed your uncle's appearance. 9. the trick; the idea. 10. just listen to me, please. 11. please to . . .; have the goodness to ... 12. is at; stops at. 13. waiting for us. (oder Anm. 12 u. 13 the postchaise is waiting for us at the door).

Garnison heimlich verlassen! Wir sind beordert, Sie stehen=
den Fußes[1] in den Wagen zu packen und nach Straßburg
zurückzubringen.

Oberst. Und das ist wieder ein[2] Streich von diesem
verwünschten Taugenichts[3]! Ha, Lotterbube!

Champagne. Ja, gnädiger Herr, es ist meine Ver=
anstaltung — Sie wissen, wie sehr ich dawider war, daß
Sie Straßburg ohne Urlaub verließen[4].

Oberst (hebt den Stock auf[5]). Nein, ich halte mich nicht
mehr[6].

Beide Unteroffiziere. Mäßigen Sie sich[7], Herr
von Dorsigny!

Champagne. Halten Sie ihn[8], meine Herren! ich
bitte — das hat man davon[9], wenn man Undankbare[10]
verpflichtet. Ich rette vielleicht Ihr Leben, da ich diesem
unseligen Duell vorbeuge[11], und zum Dank[12] hätten Sie
mich tot gemacht, wenn diese Herren nicht so gut[13] gewesen
wären, es zu verhindern.

Oberst. Was ist hier zu thun, Lormeuil?

Lormeuil. Warum berufen Sie sich nicht auf die
Personen, die Sie kennen müssen?

Oberst. An wen, zum Teufel! soll ich mich wenden[14]?
Meine Frau, meine Tochter ·sind ausgegangen — meine
Nichte ist vom[15] Komplott — die ganze Welt ist behext.

Lormeuil. So bleibt nichts übrig, als[16] (in Gottes

---

1. immediately; on the spot. 2. another. 3. scamp. 4. how
much I was against your quitting St. without leave. 5. raising
(lifting up) his stick. 6. I can't restrain myself any longer.
7. calm (moderate) yourself. 8. stop him. 9. that's all the reward one gets. 10. the ungrateful. 11. by preventing. 12. for
my pains. 13. so kind as to . . . 14. I don't know whom on
earth I could appeal (apply) to; hang it! whom shall I (am I to)
appeal (apply) to. 15. in the. 16. then there is no alternative
left but . . .

Namen] nach Straßburg zu reisen, wenn diese Leute nicht mit sich reden lassen[1].

Oberst. Das wäre aber ganz verwünscht[2].

Erster Unteroffizier (zu Champagne). Sind Sie aber auch ganz gewiß, daß es der Neffe ist?

Champagne. Freilich! Freilich! Der Onkel ist weit weg — nur standgehalten[3]! Nicht gewankt[4]!

Dritter Auftritt.
Ein Postillon. Vorige.

Postillon (betrunken). He! Holla! Wird's bald[5], ihr Herren? Meine Pferde stehen schon eine Stunde vor dem Hause[6], und ich bin nicht des Wartens wegen da[7].

Oberst. Was will der Bursch?

Erster Unteroffizier. Es ist der Postillon, der Sie fahren soll.

Postillon. Sieh doch[8]! Sind Sie's, Herr Hauptmann, der abreist? — Sie haben kurze Geschäfte hier gemacht[9]. — Heute abend kommen Sie an, und in der Nacht geht's wieder fort[10].

Oberst. Woher[11] weißt denn du?

Postillon. Ei! Ei! War ich's denn nicht, der Sie vor etlichen Stunden an der Hinterthür dieses Hauses absetzte? Sie sehen, [mein] Kapitän, daß ich Ihr Geld wohl angewendet — ja, ja, wenn mir einer was zu vertrinken gibt, so erfüll' ich gewissenhaft und redlich die[12] Absicht. —

---

1. will not (won't) listen to reason. 2. that would be highly unpleasant (deuced awkward, 'pon my word). 3. keep firm; don't budge. 4. don't vacillate (waver). 5. how long will you keep me waiting. 6. have been at the door this whole hour. 7. I didn't come here to cool my heels in the street (*slang* für to be kept waiting). 8. look there; indeed. 9. you've made short work here; you haven't let much grass grow under your feet. 10. off you are again. 11. how. 12. his.

Oberſt. Was ſagſt du, Kerl? Mich hätteſt du ge=
jahren[1]? Mich?

Poſtillon. Sie, Herr! — Ja doch, beim Teufel[2],
und da ſteht ja Ihr Bedienter, der den Vorreiter machte[3]
— Gott grüß' dich, Gaudieb[4]! Eben der hat mir's ja im
Vertrauen geſteckt[5], daß Sie ein Herr Hauptmann ſeien
und von Straßburg heimlich nach Paris gingen.

Oberſt. Wie Schurke? Ich wäre das geweſen[6]?

Poſtillon. Ja, Sie! Und der auf dem ganzen
Wege laut mit ſich ſelbſt ſprach und in einem fort[7] rief:
Meine Sophie! Mein liebes Bäschen! Mein engliſches
Couſinchen[8]! Wie? haben Sie das ſchon vergeſſen?

Champagne (zum Oberſten). Ich bin's nicht[9], gnädiger
Herr, der ihm dieſe Worte in den Mund legt. — Wer
wird aber auch[10] auf öffentlicher Poſtſtraße ſo laut von
ſeiner Gebieterin reden?

Oberſt. Es iſt beſchloſſen, ich ſeh's[11], ich ſoll nach[12]
Straßburg, um der Sünden meines Neffen willen —

Erſter Unteroffizier. Alſo, mein Herr Haupt=
mann[13] —

Oberſt. Alſo, mein Herr Geleitsmann, alſo muß ich
freilich mit Ihnen fort[14]; aber ich kann Sie verſichern,
ſehr[15] wider meinen Willen.

Erſter Unteroffizier. Das ſind wir gewohnt,
[mein] Kapitän, die Leute wider ihren Willen zu bedienen.

---

1. you pretend to have driven me here. 2. to be sure, I
did, by Jove. 3. who was the outrider. 4. how are you, old
scamp (rascal, scoundrel). 5. he it was who told me in confidence (it was him who . . . iſt gram. unrichtig, aber ſehr ge=
bräuchlich, beſonders im Volksmunde). 6. I had been that person.
7. continually; incessantly; unceasingly. 8. my angelic little cousin.
9. 'tisn't me = it is not I. cf. Anm. 5. 10. but who would be
so imprudent as to . . . 11. I see. 12. I am to go. 13. well then,
captain. 14. so I see I must certainly go with you. 15. very
much; greatly.

Oberſt. Du biſt alſo[1] mein Bedienter?

Champagne. Ja, gnädiger Herr.

Oberſt. Folglich bin ich dein Gebieter.

Champagne. Das verſteht ſich[2].

Oberſt. Ein Bedienter muß ſeinem Herrn folgen du gehſt mit mir nach Straßburg.

Champagne (für ſich). Verflucht[3]!

Poſtillon. Das verſteht ſich — marſch[4]!

Champagne. Es thut mir leid, Sie zu betrüben, gnädiger Herr — Sie wiſſen, wie groß meine Anhänglich= keit an[5] Sie iſt — ich gebe Ihnen eine ſtarke Probe da= von in[6] dieſem Augenblicke — aber Sie wiſſen auch, wie ſehr[7] ich mein Weib liebe. Ich habe ſie heute nach einer ſehr langen Trennung wiedergeſehen! Die arme Frau be= zeigte eine ſo herzliche[8] Freude über meine Zurückkunft, daß ich beſchloſſen habe, ſie nie wieder zu verlaſſen und meinen Abſchied[9] von Ihnen zu begehren. Sie werden ſich erinnern, daß Sie mir noch von drei Monaten die Gage[10] ſchuldig ſind.

Oberſt. Dreihundert Stockprügel[11] bin ich dir ſchul= dig, Bube!

Erſter Unteroffizier. [Herr] Käpitän, Sie haben kein Recht, dieſen ehrlichen Diener wider ſeinen Willen nach Straßburg mitzunehmen, und wenn Sie ihm noch Rückſtand ſchuldig ſind[12] —

Oberſt. Nichts, keinen Heller bin ich ihm ſchuldig[13].

Erſter Unteroffizier. So iſt das kein Grund, ihn mit Prügeln abzulohnen.

---

1. then you are. 2. of course. 3. dash it; blow it; con- found it. 4. off with you. 5. to. 6 at. 7. sincerely. 8. so much (such) heartfelt... 9. discharge. 10. three months' wages. 11 three hundred stripes (cuts with a stick). 12. and if you owe him still an arrear of wages. 13. not one farthing do I owe him.

Cormeuil. Ich muß sehen, wie ich ihm heraushelfe. — Wenn es nicht anders ist[1] — in Gottes Namen reisen Sie ab, Herr von Dorsigny[2]. Zum Glück bin ich frei. Ich habe Freunde, ich eile, sie in Bewegung zu setzen[3], und bringe Sie zurück, eh es Tag wird[4].

Oberst. Und ich will den Postillon [dafür] bezahlen, daß er so langsam fährt als möglich[5], damit Sie[6] mich noch einholen können. (Zum Postillon.) Hier, Schwager! Ver= trink das auf meine Gesundheit[7] — aber du mußt mich fahren —

Postillon (treuherzig). Daß die Pferde dampfen.

Oberst. Nicht doch! nein[8]! so mein' ich's nicht[9] —

Postillon. Ich will Sie fahren, wie auf[10] dem Her= weg! Als ob der Teufel Sie davonführte[11].

Oberst. Hole der Teufel dich selbst, du verdammter Trunkenbold! Ich sage dir ja —

Postillon. Sie haben's eilig[12]! Ich auch[13]! Sei'n Sie ganz ruhig[14]! Fort soll's gehen[15], daß die Funken hinausfliegen. (ab.)

Oberst (ihm nach)[16]. Der Kerl macht[17] mich rasend! Warte doch, höre[18]!

Cormeuil. Beruhigen Sie sich! Ihre Reise soll nicht lange dauern.

Oberst. Ich glaube, die ganze Hölle ist heute los= gelassen[19]. (Geht ab. Der erste Unteroffizier folgt.)

---

1. if nothing can be done; if things must take their course. 2. M. de D., by all means depart. 3. I'll hasten to stir them up. 4. before sunrise. 5. to drive as slow (slowly) as possible. 6. so that you. 7. spend this in drinking my health. 8. no, no. 9. that's not what I mean; I don't mean that. 10. as I did on . . . 11. as though (as if) the devil himself was handling the ribbons. 12. you are in a hurry. 13. so am I. 14. make your mind easy. 15. I'll drive you; we'll get along. 16. following him. 17. drives. 18. wait and listen to me, d'ye hear. 19. all the demons of h— are let loose to-day.

Lormeuil (zum zweiten). Kommen Sie, mein Herr, folgen Sie mir, weil es Ihnen so befohlen ist[1] — aber ich sage Ihnen vorher[2], ich werde Ihre Beine nicht schonen! Und wenn Sie sich Rechnung gemacht haben, diese Nacht zu schlafen[3], so sind Sie garstig betrogen[4], denn wir werden immer auf der Straße sein.

Zweiter Unteroffizier. Nach Ihrem Gefallen[5], gnädiger Herr. — Zwingen Sie sich ganz und gar nicht[6]. — Ihr Diener, Herr Champagne.

(Lormeuil und der zweite Unteroffizier ab).

Vierter Auftritt.

Champagne. Dann Frau von Mirville.

Champagne (allein). Sie sind fort[7] — Glück zu[8], Champagne! Der Sieg ist unser! Jetzt frisch ans Werk, daß wir die Heirat noch in dieser Nacht zu stande bringen[9]. — Da kommt die Schwester meines Herrn; ihr kann ich alles sagen.

Fr. v. Mirville. Ah, bist du da, Champagne? Weißt du nicht, wo der Onkel ist?

Champagne. Auf dem Wege nach Straßburg.

Fr. v. Mirville. Wie? Was? Erkläre dich!

Champagne. Recht gern, Ihr Gnaden. Sie wissen vielleicht nicht, daß mein Herr und dieser Lormeuil einen heftigen Zank zusammen gehabt haben.

Fr. v. Mirville. Ganz im Gegenteil[10]. Sie sind als die besten Freunde geschieden[11], das weiß ich.

---

1. since you have orders to do so. 2. beforehand. 3. on sleeping (on getting a wink of sleep) to-night. 4. you'll be badly (thoroughly, awfully) disappointed. 5. as you please (like). 6. don't put the least restraint on your feelings. 7. they are gone; off they are; gone they are. 8. good luck to you. 9. to bring about. 10. on the contrary; quite the contrary; quite the reverse. 11. they parted as the best of friends (on the very best terms).

Champagne. Nun, [so] habe ich's aber nicht gewußt. Und in der Hitze meines Eifers ging ich [hin], mir bei der Polizei Hülfe zu suchen[1]. Ich komme her mit zwei Ser= geanten, davon der eine Befehl hat[2], dem Herrn von Lor= meuil an der Seite[3] zu bleiben, der andere, meinen Herrn nach Straßburg zurückzubringen. Nun reitet[4] der Teufel diesen verwünschten Sergeanten, daß er den Onkel für den Neffen nimmt, ihn beinahe mit Gewalt in die Kutsche packt[5] und fort mit ihm[6], jagst du nicht, so gilt's nicht[7], nach Straßburg!

Fr. v. Mirville. Wie, Champagne! du schickst meinen Onkel anstatt meines Bruders auf die Reise! Nein, das kann nicht dein Ernst sein[8].

Champagne. Um[9] Vergebung, es ist mein voller[10] Ernst. Das Elsaß ist ein scharmantes Land; der Herr Oberst haben sich noch nicht darin umgesehen[11], und ich ver= schaffe ihm diese kleine Ergötzlichkeit.

Fr. v. Mirville. Du kannst noch scherzen? Was macht[12] aber der Herr von Lormeuil?

Champagne. Er führt seinen Sergeanten in der Stadt spazieren[13].

Fr. v. Mirville. Der arme Junge! Er verdient wohl[14], daß ich Anteil an ihm nehme[15].

Champagne. Nun, gnädige Frau! Ans Werk[16]! Keine Zeit verloren[17]! Wenn mein Herr seine Cousine

---

1. I went and applied to the police for help (assistance).
2. one of whom had orders. 3. close by the side of. 4. induces; causes. 5. puts him almost by force into the coach; places him in the coach almost by main force. 6. and away (off) they go. 7. helter-skelter. 8. no, you can't be in earnest about that. 9. begging your ... 10. I'm quite in ... 11. the colonel hasn't yet enjoyed the pleasure of catching a glimpse of it. 12. is doing. 13. he takes his sergeant out for a stroll about the town. 14. indeed. 15. that I should feel sympathy for him. 16. to business. 17. we've no time to lose.

nur erst[1] geheiratet hat, so wollen wir den Onkel zurückholen. Ich suche meinen Herrn auf; ich bringe ihn her,
und wenn nur Sie[2] uns beistehen, so muß diese Nacht
alles richtig werden[3]. (ab.)

Fünfter Auftritt.

Frau von Mirville. Dann Frau von Dorsigny.
Sophie.

Fr. v. Mirville. Das ist ein verzweifelter Bube;
aber er hat seine Sache so gut gemacht[4], daß ich mich mit
ihm verstehen muß[5]. — Hier kommt meine Tante; ich muß
ihr[6] die Wahrheit verbergen.

Fr. v. Dorsigny. Ach, liebe Nichte! Hast du deinen
Onkel nicht gesehen?

Fr. v. Mirville. Wie? Hat er denn nicht Abschied
von Ihnen[7] genommen.

Fr. v. Dorsigny. Abschied? Wie?

Fr. v. Mirville. Ja, er ist fort.

Fr. v. Dorsigny. Er ist fort? Seit wann?

Fr. v. Mirville. Diesen Augenblick.

Fr. v. Dorsigny. Das begreif' ich nicht. Er wollte
ja erst gegen elf Uhr wegfahren[8]. Und wo ist er denn
hin, so eilig[9]?

Fr. v. Mirville. Das weiß ich nicht. Ich sah ihn
nicht abreisen, Champagne erzählte mir's[10].

---

1. as soon as . . . 2. and provided you . . . 3. all will
be brought to a happy issue to-night. 4. he has acted (played)
his part so well. 5. that I must continue to act in collusion (in
covert agreement) with him. 6. from her. 7. of you. 8. he said
he didn't intend starting (leaving) before eleven. 9. where did
he go to in such a hurry (in such haste). 10. informed (told)
me of it.

Sechster Auftritt.

Die Vorigen. Franz von Dorsigny in seiner eigenen Uniform und ohne Perücke. Champagne.

Champagne. Da ist er, Ihr Gnaden, da ist er!

Fr. v. Dorsigny. Wer? mein Mann?

Champagne. Nein, nicht doch[1]! Mein Herr, der Herr Hauptmann.

Sophie (ihm entgegen[2]) Lieber Vetter!

Champagne. Ja, er hatte wohl recht, zu sagen[3], daß er mit seinem Briefe zugleich[4] eintreffen werde.

Fr. v. Dorsigny. Mein Mann reist ab, mein Neffe kommt an! Wie schnell sich die Begebenheiten drängen[5]!

Dorsigny. Seh' ich Sie endlich wieder, beste Tante. Ich komme voll Unruhe und Erwartung —

Fr. v. Dorsigny. Guten Abend, lieber Neffe!

Dorsigny. Welcher frostige Empfang?

Fr. v. Dorsigny. Ich bin herzlich erfreut, dich zu sehen. Aber mein Mann — .

Dorsigny. Ist dem Onkel etwas zugestoßen?

Fr. v. Mirville. Der Onkel ist heute abend[6] von einer großen Reise zurückgekommen, und in diesem Augen= blicke verschwindet er wieder, ohne daß wir wissen, wo er hin ist[7].

Dorsigny. Das ist ja sonderbar!

Champagne. Es ist ganz zum Erstaunen!

Fr. v. Dorsigny. Da ist ja Champagne! Der kann uns allen aus dem Traume helfen[8].

---

1. no, not quite (not exactly). 2. advancing towards him. 3. when he said (wrote). 4. together with his letter. 5. how quickly events crowd one upon another. 6. to-night. 7. and this moment he's gone away without our knowing whither, (and we know not where he's gone to). 8. he can explain the mystery to us all.

Champagne. Ich, gnädige Frau?

Fr. v. Mirville. Ja, du! Mit dir allein hat der Onkel ja gesprochen, wie er abreiste.

Champagne, Das ist wahr! Mit mir allein hat er gesprochen.

Dorsigny. Nun, so sage mir, warum verreiste er so plötzlich?

Champagne. Warum? Ei, er mußte wohl[1]! Er hatte ja Befehl dazu[2] von der Regierung.

Fr. v. Dorsigny. Was?

Champagne. Er hat einen wichtigen geheimen Auf= trag, der die größte Eilfertigkeit erfordert — der einen Mann erfordert — einen Mann — Ich sage nichts mehr[3]! Aber Sie können sich etwas darauf einbilden[4], gnädige Frau, daß die Wahl auf den Herrn gefallen ist.

Fr. v. Mirville. Allerdings! Eine solche Auszeich= nung[5] ehrt die ganze Familie!

Champagne. Euer Gnaden begreifen wohl[6], daß er sich da nicht lange mit Abschiednehmen aufhalten konnte[7]. Champagne, sagte er zu mir, ich gehe in wichtigen Staats= angelegenheiten nach — nach St. Petersburg. Der Staat befiehlt, ich muß gehorchen — beim ersten Postwechsel schreib' ich meiner Frau — was übrigens die Heirat zwischen meinem Neffen und meiner Tochter betrifft[8] — so weiß sie, daß ich vollkommen damit zufrieden bin.

Dorsigny. Was hör' ich! mein lieber Onkel sollte —

Champagne. Ja, gnädiger Herr! er willigt ein. — Ich gebe meiner Frau unumschränkte Vollmacht, sagte

---

1. he was obliged to; he couldn't help it. 2. to do so. 3. I won't say another word. 4. you may, indeed, be proud. 5. such a mark of distinction. 6. can well imagine (easily under- stand). 7. that he hadn't much time to spare for . . .; that he couldn't be much bothered by . . . 8. however, as to the marri- age between . . .

er, alles zu beendigen, und ich hoffe, bei meiner Zurückkunft unsere Tochter als eine glückliche Frau zu finden.

Fr. v. Dorsigny. Und so reiste er allein ab?

Champagne. Allein? Nicht doch[1]! Er hatte noch einen Herrn bei sich[2], der nach etwas recht Vornehmem aus= sah[3]. —

Fr. v. Dorsigny. Ich kann mich gar nicht drein finden[4].

Fr. v. Mirville. Wir wissen seinen Wunsch. Man muß dahin sehen[5], daß er sie als Mann und Frau[6] findet bei[7] seiner Zurückkunft.

Sophie. Seine Einwilligung scheint mir nicht im geringsten zweifelhaft, und ich trage gar kein[8] Bedenken, den Vetter auf der Stelle zu heiraten.

Fr. v. Dorsigny. Aber ich trage Bedenken[9] — und will seinen ersten Brief noch abwarten.

Champagne (beiseite). Da sind wir nun schön ge= fördert[10], daß wir den Onkel nach Petersburg schicken[11]

Dorsigny. Aber beste Tante!

Siebenter Auftritt.
Die Vorigen. Der Notarius.

Notar (tritt zwischen Dorsigny und seine Tante). Ich empfehle mich der ganzen hochgeneigten Gesellschaft zu Gnaden[12].

Fr. v. Dorsigny. Sieh da, Herr Gaspar, der No= tar unseres Hauses.

---

1. not at all. 2. there was another gentleman with him. 3. who looked rather distinguished; (who looked a great swell, *slang*). 4. I can't quite see my way; I can't make head or tail of it. 5. we must take care. 6. as husband and wife. 7. on. 8. not the slightest (least). 9. but I have some doubts. 10. there we are in a nice fix. 11. after sending . . . Anm. 10 u. 11. botheration! much good, it seems, we are going to derive from sending the uncle to St. Petersburgh. 12. to the favour of this most honourable company present.

Notar. Zu Dero Befehl[1], gnädige Frau! Es beliebte Dero Herrn Gemahl, sich in mein Haus zu verfügen[2].

Fr. v. Dorsigny. Wie[3]? Mein Mann wäre vor seiner Abreise noch bei Ihnen gewesen[4]?

Notar. Vor Dero[5] Abreise! Was Sie mir sagen[6]! Sieh, sieh doch[7]! Darum hatten es der gnädige Herr so eilig[8] und wollten mich gar nicht[9] in meinem Hause erwarten. Dieses Billet ließen mir Hochdieselben zurück[10]. — Belieben Ihro Gnaden[11] es durchzulesen. (Reicht der Frau von Dorsigny das Billet.)

Champagne (leise zu Dorsigny). Da ist der Notar, den Ihr Onkel bestellt hat.

Dorsigny. Ja, wegen Lormeuil's Heirat.

Champagne (leise). Wenn wir ihn zu der Ihrigen gebrauchen könnten[12]?

Dorsigny. Stille! Hören wir[13], was er schreibt!

Fr. v. Dorsigny (liest): „Haben Sie die Güte, mein „Herr, sich noch diesen Abend in mein Haus zu bemühen[14] „und den Ehekontrakt mitzubringen[15], den Sie für meine „Tochter aufgesetzt haben. Ich habe meine Ursachen[16], diese „Heirat noch in dieser Nacht[17] abzuschließen. — Dorsigny."

Champagne. Da haben wir's schwarz auf weiß[18]! Nun wird die gnädige Frau doch nicht mehr an der Einwilligung des Herrn Onkels zweifeln[19]?

---

1. at your service. 2. to call at my house. 3. what. 4. has been to see you . . . 5. his. 6. you don't say so. 7. well, look now. 8. that's why his honour (his grace) was in such a hurry. 9. and would not . . . 10. he deigned (condescended, was pleased) to leave me this note. 11. be pleased to; may it please your honour to. 12. if we could (suppose we were to) use him for yours. 13. let us hear. . 14. Sir, be so kind as to call at my house to-night (this evening). 15. and bring with you. 16. I've good reasons (my reasons) for, mit pres. part. 17. this very night. 18. there we've got it in black and white. 19. now, my lady will surely have no longer any doubt about . . .

Sophie. Es ist also gar nicht nötig, daß der Papa Ihnen schreibt[1], liebe Mutter, da er diesem Herrn geschrieben hat.

Fr. v. Dorsigny. Was denken Sie von der Sache[2], Herr Gaspar?

Notar. Nun, dieser Brief wäre[3] deutlich genug, dächt' ich.

Fr. v. Dorsigny. In Gottes Namen, meine Kinder[4]. Seid glücklich! — Gebt euch die Hände[5], weil[6] mein Mann selbst den Notar herschickt[7]!

Dorsigny. Frisch, Champagne! Einen Tisch, Feder und Tinte; wir wollen gleich unterzeichnen.

Achter Auftritt.

Oberst Dorsigny. Dalcour. Vorige

Fr. v. Mirville. Himmel[8]! Der Onkel!

Sophie. Mein Vater!

Champagne. Führt ihn der Teufel zurück?

Dorsigny. Jawohl, der Teufel[9]! Dieser Balcour ist mein böser Genius.

Fr. v. Dorsigny. Was seh' ich? Mein Mann!

Dalcour (den älteren Dorsigny präsentierend). Wie schätz' ich mich glücklich[10], einen geliebten Neffen in den Schoß seiner Familie zurückführen zu können[11]! (Wie er den jüngeren Dorsigny gewahr wird.) Wie[12], Teufel, da bist du ja — (Sich zum älteren Dorsigny wendend.) Und wer sind Sie denn, mein Herr?

---

1. that papa should write to you; for papa to write to you. 2. what's your view of (opinion about) the matter. 3. is. 4. all right, then, my dear children (in heaven's name . . .) 5. join hands. 6. since. 7. has sent. 8. good gracious. 9. yes indeed, he does. 10. how happy (glad) I am. 11. to be able to restore a beloved nephew to the bosom of his family. 12. but, the deuce, there you are already.

Oberſt. Sein Onkel, mein Herr.

Dorſigny. Aber erkläre mir, Valcour —

Valcour. Erkläre du mir ſelbſt! Ich bringe in Er=
fahrung, daß eine Ordre ausgefertigt ſei, dich nach deiner
Garniſon zurückzuſchicken. Nach unſäglicher Mühe erlange
ich, daß ſie widerrufen wird[1]. Ich werfe mich aufs Pferd[2],
ich erreiche noch bald genug die Poſtchaiſe, wo ich dich zu
finden glaubte und finde auch wirklich[3] —

Oberſt. Ihren gehorſamen Diener, fluchend und tobend
über[4] einen verwünſchten Poſtknecht, dem ich Geld gegeben
hatte, um mich langſam zu fahren, und der mich wie ein
Sturmwind davonführte[5].

Valcour. Dein Herr Onkel findet es nicht für gut[6],
mich aus meinem Irrtum zu reißen[7]; die Poſtchaiſe lenkt
wieder um, nach Paris zurück, und da bin ich [nun]. Ich
hoffe, du kannſt dich nicht über meinen Eifer beklagen.

Dorſigny. Sehr[8] verbunden, mein Freund, für die
mächtigen Dienſte, die du mir geleiſtet haſt! Es thut mir
nur leid um die unendliche Mühe[9], die du dir gegeben haſt.

Oberſt. Herr von Valcour! Mein Neffe erkennt
Ihre große Güte vielleicht nicht mit der gehörigen[10] Dank=
barkeit; aber rechnen Sie [dafür] auf die meinige.

Fr. v. Dorſigny. Sie waren alſo nicht unterwegs
nach Rußland?

Oberſt. Was Teufel ſollte ich[11] in Rußland?

Fr. v. Dorſigny. Nun wegen der wichtigen Kom=

---

1. I obtain its recall. 2. I mount my horse with the utmost
speed. 3. in reality. 4. at. 5. who drove (carried) me along
with the swiftness of the wind. 6. your uncle does not think
proper. 7. to undeceive (enlighten) me; to explain to me the
whole affair. 8. very much; greatly; extremely; (awfully, *slang*).
9. I'm only sorry (that) you should have taken such infinite pains.
10. with becoming. 11. what the deuce should I do . . .

miſſion, die das Ministerium Ihnen auftrug[1], wie Sie dem Champagne ſagten.

Oberſt. Alſo[2] wieder der Champagne, der mich zu dieſem hohen Poſten befördert. Ich bin ihm unendlichen Dank ſchuldig, daß er ſo hoch mit mir hinaus will[3]. — Herr Gaspar, Sie werden zu Hauſe mein Billet gefunden haben[4]; es würde mir lieb ſein, wenn der Ehekontrakt noch dieſe Nacht unterzeichnet würde[5].

Notar. Nichts iſt leichter[6], gnädiger Herr! Wir waren eben im Begriff, dieſes Geſchäft auch in Ihrer Ab= weſenheit vorzunehmen[7].

Oberſt. Sehr wohl! Man verheiratet ſich zuweilen[8] ohne den Vater; aber wie[9] ohne den Bräutigam, das iſt mir doch nie vorgekommen[10].

Fr. v. Dorſigny. Hier iſt der Bräutigam! Unſer lieber Neffe!

Dorſigny. Ja, beſter Onkel! Ich bin's.

Oberſt. Mein Neffe iſt ein ganz hübſcher Junge[11]; aber meine Tochter bekommt er nicht[12].

Fr. v. Dorſigny. Nun, wer ſoll ſie denn ſonſt be= kommen[13]?

Oberſt. Wer, fragen Sie[14]? Zum Henker[15]! Der Herr von Lormeuil ſoll ſie bekommen.

---

1. why, on account of the important commission the ministry entrusted you with. 2. so it is. 3. for desiring to promote me to so high a post of honour. 4. I suppose you found. 5. could (would, were to) be signed this very night. 6. nothing more easy. 7. of proceeding with this business. 8. people some- times marry; a wedding sometimes takes place; a marriage is sometimes concluded. 9. but how this can be done. 10. I never heard of before. 11. a very nice youth (young man). 12. he won't get (he shan't marry) . . . 13. well, who else is to marry (shall have) her. 14. who, you ask. 15. why, to be sure; of course.

Fr. v. Dorsigny. Er ist also nicht tot, der[1] Herr von Lormeuil?

Oberst. Nicht doch[2], Madame! Er lebt, er ist hier. Sehen Sie sich nur um[3], dort kommt er.

Fr. v. Dorsigny. Und wer ist denn der Herr[4], der mit ihm ist?

Oberst. Das ist ein Kammerdiener, den Herr Champagne beliebt hat, ihm an die Seite zu geben[5].

Neunter Auftritt.

Die Vorigen. Lormeuil mit seinem Unteroffizier, der sich im Hintergrunde[6] des Zimmers niedersetzt.

Lormeuil (zum Obersten). Sie schicken also[7] Ihren Onkel an Ihrer Statt[8] nach Straßburg! Das wird Ihnen nicht so hingehen, mein Herr[9].

Oberst. Sieh, sieh doch[10]! Wenn du dich ja mit Gewalt schlagen willst[11], Lormeuil, so schlage dich mit[12] meinem Neffen und nicht mit mir.

Lormeuil (erkennt ihn). Wie? Sind Sie's? Und wie haben Sie's gemacht, daß Sie[13] so schnell zurückkommen?

Oberst. Hier, bei diesem Herrn von Valcour bedanken Sie sich[14], der mich aus Freundschaft für meinen Neffen spornstreichs zurückholte.

Dorsigny. Ich begreife Sie nicht, Herr von Lor-

---

1. he is not dead then, this. 2. not at all; by no means. 3. just you look round for a moment. 4. the gentleman. 5. whom Mr. Ch. has been pleased to give (to select for) him as his attendant. 6. at the back. 7. so you send. 8. in your place (stead). 9. that shall not be passed over so lightly, sir. 10. look you, sir. 11. if you absolutely insist on fighting a duel. 12. fight (go out) with. 13. and how did you manage to . . . 14. here, you may thank this . . .

meuil. Wir waren ja als bie besten Freunde voneinander geschieden[1]. Haben Sie mir nicht selbst, noch ganz kürz= lich[2], alle Ihre Ansprüche auf[3] die Hand meiner Cousine abgetreten[4]?

Oberst. Nichts, nichts! Daraus wird nichts[5]! Meine Frau, meine Tochter, meine Nichte, mein Neffe, alle zusammen sollen mich nicht hindern, meinen. Willen durchzusetzen[6].

Cormeuil. Herr von Dorsigny! Mich freut's von Herzen[7], daß Sie von einer Reise zurück sind, die Sie wider Ihren Willen angetreten[8]. Aber wir haben gut reden und Heiratspläne schmieden[9], Fräulein Sophie wird barum boch[10] Ihren Neffen lieben.

Oberst. Ich verstehe nichts von diesem allem[11]! Aber ich werde den Cormeuil nicht von Toulon nach Paris gesprengt haben, daß er als ein Junggesell zurück= kehren soll[12].

Dorsigny. Was das betrifft[13] mein Onkel — so ließe sich vielleicht eine Auskunft treffen[14], daß Herr von Cormeuil keinen vergeblichen Weg gemacht hätte[15]. — Fragen Sie meine Schwester.

---

1. we had parted as the best of friends. 2. quite lately. 3. to. 4. to cede, to surrender, to resign (to me). 5. nothing of the sort, that won't do at all. 6. from carrying my point; from having my way; from enforcing my will. 7. I am heartily rejoiced (glad). 8. from the trip (journey) you took against your will. 9. but for all our talking and match-making; in spite of all our etc. 10. nevertheless; all the same. 11. I don't understand a word of all this. 12. but after inducing L. to hurry up from T. to P. with all speed, I won't allow his re- turning home as a bachelor; but I should not like to have hurried up L. from T. to P., and that he should return etc. 13. as to that. 14. an arrangement might perhaps be made. 15. so that M. de L. should not have come here in vain.

Fr. v. Mirville. Mich? Ich habe nichts zu sagen.

Cormeuil. Nun, so will ich denn reden[1]. Herr von Dorsigny, Ihre Nichte ist frei; bei der Freund= schaft, davon Sir mir noch heute einen so großen Be= weis geben wollten[2], bitte ich Sie, verwenden Sie allen Ihren Einfluß bei[3] Ihrer Nichte, daß sie es übernehmen möge, Ihre Wortbrüchigkeit gegen mich gutzumachen.

Oberst. Was? Wie? — Ihr sollt ein Paar wer= den[4] — und dieser Schelm, der Champagne, soll mir für alle zusammen bezahlen.

Champagne. Gott soll mich verdammen[5], gnädiger Herr, wenn ich nicht selbst zuerst von der Ähnlichkeit be= trogen wurde. — Verzeihen Sie mir die kleine Spazier= fahrt, die ich Sie machen ließ[6]! Es geschah meinem Herrn zum Besten[7].

Oberst (zu beiden Paaren). Nun, so unterzeichnet!

---

1. well, then I will speak. 2. which you desired (wanted) to give me so signal a proof of this very day. 3. with. 4. you two shall be united. 5. I'll be hanged (confounded, cursed). 6. the little trip (drive, journey) I made you take. 7. it was all done for the good (in the interest) of my master.

Wörterverzeichnis.

Erklärung der Abkürzungen.

a. adjective, Eigenschaftswort. adv. adverb, Umstandswort. c. conjunction, Bindewort. f. feminine gender, weiblichen Geschlechts. i. interjection, Empfindungswort. m. masculine gender, männlichen Geschlechts. n. neuter gender, sächlichen Geschlechts. p. participle, Participium. pl. plural, Mehrzahl. prn. pronoun, Fürwort. prp. preposition, Verhältniswort. v. a. verb active, transitives Zeitwort. v. imp. verb impersonal, unpersönliches Zeitwort. v. n. verb neuter, intransitives Zeitwort. v. r. verb reflexive, zurückführendes Zeitwort.

ab, adv. off; — von der Bühne, exit, pl. exeunt.

Abend, m. evening; heute abend, this evening, to-night.

Abenteuer, n. adventure.

aber, c. but.

abholen, v. a. to go to meet

ablegen, v. a. to take off

ablohnen, v. a. to pay off.

abmachen, to settle, to arrange.

Abrede, f. counsel.

Abreise, f. departure.

abreisen, v. n. to set out, to depart.

Abschied, m. departure, leave; das —nehmen, leave-taking.

abschließen, v. a. to settle, to conclude, to ratify.

abschneiden, v. a. to cut.

absetzen, v. a. to set down.

Absicht, f. intention.

abtreten, v. a. to surrender, to resign.

abwarten, v. a. to wait for.

abweisen, v. a. to reject, to refuse, to dismiss.

abwesend, a. absent, not at home, away.

Abwesenheit, f. absence.

ach, i. ah, oh, alas. -- ja, yes indeed.

acht, eight; eighth.

ah, i. oh.

ähnlich, a. like, resembling; — sehen, to resemble.

Ähnlichkeit, f. resemblance.

Albernheit, f. nonsense, absurdity.

allein, a. alone; c. but.

allerdings, adv. to be sure, certainly, perfectly.

allerliebst, a. delightful, charming.

allgemein, a. common.

als, c. as, when; than, but; — ob, as if, as though.

alsdann, adv. then.

also, adv. and so, then; — c. therefore.

alt, a. old; älter, elder, older.

ältlich, a. old, oldish.

Amt, n. business; duty.

anbieten, v. a. to offer, to present.

Anblick, m. sight, view, look.

anbringen, v. a. to address, to offer.

ander, a. other; den —n Tag, the next day.

anders, adv. otherwise.

Anfang, m. commencement, beginning; den — machen, to begin, to commence.

anfangen, v. a. to begin.
anfangs, adv. at first.
anfechten, v. a. to disquiet.
anflehen, v. a. to implore.
anführen, v. a. to deceive.
Angelegenheit, f. concern, affair, matter.
angenehm, a. agreeable.
angreifen, v. a. to seize, to lay hold of.
Angreifer, m. aggressor
Angſt, f. fear, anxiety.
anhalten, v. a. to propose for, to sue for the hand of, to solicit.
Anhänglichkeit, f. attachment.
anhören, v. a. to listen to.
ankommen v. n. to arrive, to return.
Ankunft, f. arrival.
annehmen, v. a. to put on, to assume.
anreden, v. a. to accost.
anrichten, v. a. to cause, to make.
anſehen, v. a. to look at, upon; einen für etwas —, to take one for.
Anſpruch, m. claim; pretension.
anſtatt, prp. instead of.
anſtecken, v. a. to infect.
anſtellen, v. a. to institute, to make.
Anteil, m. compassion.
antreffen, v. a. to find.
anvertrauen, v. a. to entrust, (to intrust), to confide.
anwenden, v. a. to use, to employ; wohl —, to make good use of.
anziehen, v. n. to approach; angezogen kommen, to come, to arrive.
arg, a. arrant, arch, bad; adv sadly.
arm, a. poor.
Art, f. manner, way.
artig, a. pretty, nice.

Artikel, m. article; Heiratsartikel. pl. marriage-articles, marriage-contract, marriage-settlement.
auch, c. also; adv. even.
auf, prp. upon, on.
aufbrauſen, v. n. to fume, to storm, to rage, to fly into a violent passion.
aufbrauſend, a. hot tempered.
aufgeben, v. a. to give up.
aufhalten, v. a. to delay.
aufheben, v. a. to take up, to break off.
Aufnahme, f. welcome.
aufnehmen, v. a. to receive, to take up.
aufſchieben, v. a. to delay, to put off.
aufſetzen, v a. to draw up, to prepare.
aufſtehen, v. n. to get up.
aufſuchen, v. a. to try to find, to seek out.
Auftrag, m. commission, charge.
auftragen, v. a. to entrust (intrust) with.
auftreten, v. n. to appear.
Auftritt, m. scene.
Aufzug, m. act.
Auge, n. eye.
Augenblick, m. moment.
aus, prp. out, out of
ausbezahlen, v. a. to pay.
ausbleiben, v. n. to stay out, — away, to fail; er wird nicht lange —, he will not be long
ausdrücken, v. a. to express.
ausdrücklich, adv. expressly.
ausfertigen, v. a. to issue.
ausführbar, a. practicable.
ausgehen, v. n. to go out.
Auskunft, f. information.
ausmachen, v. a. to settle, to arrange.
ausruhen (ſich), v. r. to rest one's self.
ausſchütten, v. a. to open, to pour out.
ausſehen, v. n. to look.

Ausspruch, m. decision.
Ausstaffierung, f. equipment, disguise.
ausstehen, v. a. to endure.
aussuchen, v. a. to choose.
außerordentlich, a. extraordinary; adv. exceedingly.
Auszeichnung, f. distinction.
bald, adv. soon.
Ball, m. ball; auf einem —, at a ball.
Bankerott, m. bankruptcy, er hat — gemacht, he is a bankrupt.
barmherzig, a. gracious, merciful.
Barmherzigkeit, f. mercy, compassion.
Base, f. cousin.
bedauern, v. a. to lament; — lassen, to be very sorry.
bedenken, v. a. to consider; — Sie, recollect.
Bedenken, n. hesitation, objection.
bedeuten, v. n. to mean; zu — haben, to be important, to be of consequence.
bedienen, v. a. to wait upon.
Bediente, m. valet, servant
beendigen, v. a. to settle, to arrange, to finish, to conclude.
Befehl, m. command, order.
befehlen, v. a. to order, to command.
befinden (sich), v. r. to be.
befördern, v. a. to promote, to call.
Begebenheit, f. occurrence.
begegnen, v. a. to meet, to befall; v. n. to happen, to take place.
begehren, v. a. to ask, to request, to demand.
begleiten, v. a. to accompany.
begnügen (sich), v. r. to be contented.
begreifen, v. a. to comprehend, to understand, to make out.
Begriff, m. im —sein, to be on the point of, to be about to.
behaupten, v. a. to declare, to assert.

behexen, v. a. to bewitch.
behilflich, behülflich sein, to assist.
behüten, v. a. to preserve; Gott behüte, God forbid.
bei, prp. at, with, on, by.
beide, a. both; die —n, the two.
Beifall, m. consent, approbation.
Bein, n. leg.
beinahe, adv. almost, nearly.
beiseite, adv. aside, apart.
Beispiel, n. example, pattern.
Beistand, m. assistance.
beistehen, v. a. to assist.
bekannt, a. known; — machen, to introduce.
Bekanntschaft, f. acquaintance.
bekennen, v. a. to own, to confess.
beklagen, v. a. to pity; sich — über, to complain of.
bekommen, v. a. to get.
beleidigen, v. a. to offend, to insult.
belieben, v. a. to please; es beliebt Ihnen, you are pleased.
Belohnung, f. reward.
bemerken, v. a. to notice, to remark.
bemerklich, a. remarkable, visible.
bemühen, v. a. to trouble.
benutzen, v. a. to use.
beobachten, v. a. to observe; seine Pflicht —, to perform one's duty.
beordern, v. a. to order.
Bequemlichkeit, f. comfort.
berufen, v. a. to summon, to call; sich —, to appeal to.
beruhigen, v. a. to quiet, to calm; sich —, to calm one's self.
besänftigen, v. a. to appease.
bescheiden, v. a. to appoint.
beschließen, v. a. to settle, to determine, to decide, to resolve upon.
beschreiben, v. a. to describe.
Beschreibung, f. description.
besetzen, v. a. to occupy.
besinnen (sich), v. r. to recollect.
Besitz, m. possession; in —nehmen, to take possession of.

befitzen, v. a. to obtain, to possess.
befoffen, a. drunk.
Beforgniß, f. anxiety.
beffern, v. a. to reform, to improve.
beftellen, v. a. to send for, to order.
beft, a. best; — er Onkel, — e Tante, dearest uncle, — aunt.
beftimmen, v. a. to choose, to destine (for).
beftimmt, a. intended, destined, appointed.
Befuch, m. visit.
betrachten, v. a. to observe, to consider.
Betragen, n. conduct, behaviour.
betragen (fich), v. r. to behave, to conduct one's self.
betreffen, v. a to regard, to concern.
betrüben, v. a. to grieve; fich —, to be vexed at (about).
betrügen, v. a. to deceive.
betrunken, a. drunk, tipsy.
Bett, n. bed.
bewahren, v. a. to preserve; Gott bewahre, God (heaven) forbid.
Beweis, m. proof.
Bewegung, f. movement, motion.
bewußt, a. in question.
bezahlen, v. a. to pay.
bezeugen, v. a. to display, to show.
Billet, n. letter, note.
billig, a. moderate, reasonable.
billigen, v. a. to approve of.
bleiben, v. n. to remain, to stay.
bloß, adv. only, merely.
blühen, v. n. to bloom.
borgen, v. a. to borrow, to lend.
böfe, a. angry, bad; mein — r Geift, my evil genius.
Brauch, m. custom.
brauchen, v. a. to need, to want.
Braut, f. bride, betrothed, intended.
Brautanzug, m. wedding-dress
Bräutigam, m. bridegroom.
brennen, v. a. u. n. to burn.
Bruder, m. brother.
Bube, m. knave, villain, fellow.

Burfche, m. fellow.
C fiehe K.
da, c. as, because, since; adv. here, there.
dabei, adv. thereby; — bleiben, to stick to.
dagegen, adv. in return, on the other hand.
Dame, f. lady.
damit, c. that, in order that; adv. therewith, with it.
dampfen, v. n. to steam, to smoke.
Dankbarkeit, f. gratitude.
danken, v. a. to thank (c acc.)
darauf, adv. thereupon, afterwards.
darinnen, adv. within.
darüber, adv. about it (that), at (over) it.
dauern, v. n. to last.
davonführen, v. a. to drive.
dawiderfein, v. n. to be opposed to.
decken, v. a. to cover
Degenftich, m. sword-thrust, stab.
dein, e, —, pr. your.
denken, v. a. to think, to intend.
denn, c. for; adv. then.
der, pr. he, who.
derb, a. coarse, rude, rough.
dero, pr. your, yours; his.
defto, adv. the; — beffer, all the better, so much the better.
deutlich, a. plain clear.
dienen, v. a. to serve.
Diener, m. servant.
Dienft, m. service.
doch, c. but, however, adv. I hope, pray, please, nicht —, not so, surely not.
doppelt, a. double.
drängen, v. a. to press on.
drehen, v. a. to turn.
drei, three. dreizehnt, thirteenth.
Dreiftigkeit, f. assurance.
dringen, v. a. to press.
dringend, a. urgent.
dritt, third.
Dummkopf, m. blockhead.

Dunkelheit, f. darkness.
durchlesen, v. a. to read.
durchsetzen, v. a. to finish, to complete.
dürfen, v. n. to dare; darf ich, may I.
eben, adv. just.
ebenso adv. in the same manner.
Edelmann, m. nobleman.
ehe, eh, c. before.
Eheherr, m. husband.
Ehekontrakt, m. marriage contract.
Ehre, f. honour.
ehren, v. a. to honour.
Ehrensache, f. affair of honour.
Ehrenwort, n. word of honour.
ehrlich, a. honest.
Ehrlichkeit, f. honesty.
ei, i. well, ha, ah.
Eifer, m. zeal.
eigen, a. own.
Eile, f. hurry, haste.
eilen, v. n. to hasten, to hurry.
eilfertig, adv. hastily.
Eilfertigkeit, speed, expedition.
einander, adv. each other.
einbilden (sich etwas), v. r. to imagine, to believe.
Einbildungskraft, f. imagination.
einerlei, a. the same.
Einfall, m. idea.
einfallen, v. n. to occur to; to inspire one; es fällt mir nicht ein, I have no intention at all.
einfältig, a. silly, ridiculous.
einfinden (sich), v. r. to repair to, to call, to appear (bei = with).
Einfluß, m. influence.
einholen, v. a. to catch up, to overtake.
einig, a. one; — sein, — werden, to agree (über, on, upon, about).
einkaufen, v. a. to buy, to purchase.
einladen, v. a. to invite.
einlegen, v. a. to gain, to procure, to get.

einmal, adv. once; nicht —, not even.
einnehmen, v. a. to take.
einrichten, v. a. to arrange.
einschließen, v. a. to shut up, to closet.
eins, adv. of the same opinion; — sein, — werden, to agree.
einsehen, v. a. to see.
eintreffen, v. n. to arrive.
eintreten, v. n. to enter.
einwenden, v. a. to object (to).
einwickeln, v. a. to wrap up, to envelop.
einwilligen, v. n. to agree, to consent.
Einwilligung, f. consent.
einzig, a. single, only; sole.
elf, eleven; elft eleventh.
Elsaß, n. Alsace, Alsatia.
Empfang, m. welcome, reception.
Empfangschein, m. receipt.
empfehlen, v. a. to recommend, to commend; sich —, to recommend one's self.
Ende, n. end; zu — bringen, to finish.
Endesunterzeichnete, m. undersigned.
endlich, adv. finally, at last.
Engel, m. angel.
englisch = engelgleich, a. angelic.
Enkelchen, n. little grand child.
entdecken, v. a. to open, to discover.
entfernen, v. a. to remove.
entgegen, prp. opposed to; — sein, to oppose.
entgegengesetzt, a. opposite.
entsagen, v. a. to renounce, to give up.
entschuldigen, v. a. to excuse; sich —, to apologize.
entweder, c. either; — oder, either . . . or.
entwickeln, v. a. to explain.
Entwickelung, f. catastrophe, development.

Epidemie, f. epidemic.

Entzücken, n. delight; zum —, beautifully, enchantingly, charmingly.

erbaulich, a. comforting, edifying, refreshing.

Erbschaft, f. inheritance.

erfahren, v. a. to hear, to learn.

Erfahrung, f experience; in — bringen, to learn.

Erfindung, f. invention.

erfordern, v. a. to demand, to require.

erfreuen (sich), v. r. to rejoice.

erfreut sein, to be delighted (rejoiced).

erfüllen, v. a. to fulfil, to comply with.

ergeben, a. devoted, attached; —ster Diener, most faithful (humble) servant.

ergeben (sich), v. r. to yield, to consent.

Ergötzlichkeit, f. amusement.

ergreifen, v. a. to seize.

ergründen, v. a. to fathom, to penetrate.

erhalten, v. a. to receive.

erinnern, v. a. to remind, (an — of); sich —, to remember (c. acc.)

erkennen, v. a. to recognise, to acknowledge.

erkenntlich, a. grateful.

erklären, v. a. to state, to explain; sich —, to explain one's self.

erlangen, v. a. to obtain, to acquire.

erlauben, v. a. to allow.

Erlaubnis, f. permission.

Ernst, m. earnest, seriousness.

ernsthaft, adv. seriously.

Eroberung, f. conquest.

erraten, v. a. to guess.

erreichen, v. a. to overtake, to reach.

erschrecken, v. a. to frighten, to alarm.

erst, a. first.

erstaunen, v. n. to be astonished.

Erstaunen, n. astonishment; in — setzen, to astonish, to amaze; zum —, astonishing.

erstaunlich, a. astonishing.

erstechen, v. a. to run through with a sword, to kill.

ersuchen, v. a. to request.

ertragen, v. a. to bear.

erwarten, v. a. to wait for, to await, to expect.

Erwartung, f. expectation.

erwerben, v. a. to gain, to acquire.

erzählen, v. a. to tell, to relate.

erzeigen, v. a. to show; einen Dienst —, to render, (to do) a service.

erziehen, v. a. to bring up.

Esel, m. jackass, fool.

Eskorte, f. escort.

eskortieren, v. a. to escort.

etliche, pl. a. some, a few. few.

fähig, a capable; ready.

fahren, v. a. to drive.

Fall, m. case, situation.

fallen, v. n. to fall.

Familie, f. family.

Farbe, f. complexion.

fassen, v. a. to take.

fast, adv. scarcely, hardly, almost.

Feder, f. pen.

Fehler, m. fault.

festnehmen, v. a. to arrest.

feurig, a. passionate; adv. passionately.

Figur, f. figure.

finden, v. a. to find.

flehen, v. a. to beg.

fleißig, a. industrious.

fliehen, v. n. to flee, to fly, to run away.

fluchen, v. n. to curse (auf, at).

Flucht, f. flight, escape.

folgen, v. n. to follow.

folglich, adv. consequently.

fordern, v. a. to ask, to demand.

förbern, v. a. to advance to promote.

fort, adv. gone, away.

forteilen, v. n. to hurry off.

fortfahren, v. n. to continue.

fortreisen, v. n. to set off, to depart.

fragen, v. a. to ask.

Franz, m. Frank, Francis.

Frau, f. woman, lady; Ehefrau, wife, Mrs; Frau von D, Madame de D. ob. Mrs D.

Fräulein, n. miss, young lady.

frei, a. clear; disengaged, free.

freilich, adv. to be sure, certainly.

Freude, f. joy (über = at).

freuen (fich), v. r. to be delighted (über = at). to be glad (of).

Freund, m. friend.

Freundschaft, f. friendship.

frisch, a. u. adv. quick. — zu, quick.

frischweg, adv. quick, quickly.

frostig, a. cold, frosty.

früh, a. u. adv. early.

fügen, v. a. to unite; fich —, to chance, to happen.

führen, v. a to lead, to bear; eine Sache —, to plead a cause; einen Namen —, to bear a name.

fünf, five; fünft, fifth.

fünfzehn, fifteen.

fünfzig, fifty.

Funke, m. spark.

für, prp. for; — fich, aside.

fürchten, v. a. to fear; fich —, to be afraid of.

Fuß, m. foot; fich einem zu Füßen werfen, to fall down (to throw one's self down) at a person's feet.

Gage, f. wages.

galant, a. polite, attentive, gallant.

ganz, a. whole; adv. quite; den —en Tag, all day.

gar, adv. very; — nicht, not at all.

Garnison, f. garrison.

garstig, adv. disagreeably, badly, thoroughly.

Garten, m. garden

Gartensaal, m. drawing-room in a summer residence.

Gaudieb, m. rogue.

Gauner, m. swindler.

Gebieter, m. master.

Gebieterin, f. mistress; sweetheart, lady-love.

Gebrauch, m. use.

Geduld, f. patience.

gedulbig, a. patient, long-suffering; adv. patiently.

Geduldprobe, f. trial of patience.

Gefallen, m. favour, pleasure.

gefällig, a. obliging, kind, gentle.

gegen, prp. towards.

Gegenteil, n. contrary; im —, on the contrary.

Gegner, m. adversary.

geheim, a. secret.

Geheimniß, n. secret, mystery.

gehen, v. n. to go.

gehorchen, v. a. to obey.

gehörig, a. becoming, proper, requisite, necessary.

gehorsam, a. obedient.

Geldmäkler, m. money-broker.

gelegen, a. convenient.

Gelegenheit, f. opportunity, occasion.

Geleitsmann, m. guide, companion, conductor.

geliebt, a. beloved.

Geliebte, m. u. f. lover; mistress.

gelten, v. n. to cost, to have influence; für etwas —, to pass for.

gemach, adv. gently, softly.

Gemahl, m. husband.

Genius, m. genius.

genug, adv. enough.

gerade, a. straight; adv. just.

gerichtlich, adv. at law.

geringst, a. least; im —en, in the least.

gern, adv. willingly, gladly; recht —, right (very) willingly, with the greatest pleasure.

Geſchäft, n. business.
geſchehen, v. n. to happen.
Geſchicklichkeit, f. skill.
Geſchmack, m. taste, liking.
Geſchwätz, n. rubbish, idle talk.
geſchwind, adv. quick.
Geſchwindigkeit, f. haste; in aller
—, in the greatest haste.
Geſell, m. fellow.
Geſellſchaft, f. company, society.
geſetzt (daß), c. suppose (that).
Geſicht, n. face; mir ins —, to
my face.
geſpornt, a. spurred; geſtiefelt
und —, booted and spurred.
Geſtalt,f. appearance,shape,figure.
Geſtändnis, n. confession.
geſtehen, v. a. to confess.
Geſundheit, f. health.
gewahr werden, v. n. to become
aware of, to perceive.
Gewaltthätigkeit, f. violence.
gewinnen, v. a. to gain, to win
gewiß, a. certain, sure; adv. —ly.
Gewiſſen, n. conscience.
gewiſſenhaft, a. conscientious;
adv. —ly.
Gewohnheit, f. habit.
gewohnt ſein, v. n. to be accusto-
med to.
glauben, v. a. to think, to expect.
gleich, a. equal, like; adv. = ſogleich),
immediately, at once, quickly.
gleichen, v. a. to resemble.
Glück, n. luck: zum —, luckily.
glücken, v. n. to succeed.
glücklich, a. lucky, happy, successful, safe, prosperous.
Gnade, f. grace, pity, favour.
Euer —n, Your Grace.
gnädig, a. gracious; meine Gnädige, my lady, Your Grace
(doch) nur zu hochadligen Damen,
ſonſt Madam) —er Herr, my
lord, your honour; —e Frau,
my lady, your honour.
Gott, God; mein —, good gra-

cious; ach —, good heavens.
— ſei Dank, heaven be praised.
grauſam, a. cruel, terrible.
greifen, v. a. to seize.
Grimaſſe, f. grimace.
Groll, m. animosity, ill will.
groß, a. great.
Größe, f. height, size.
großmütig, a. magnanimous; adv.
—ly, graciously.
grüßen, v. a. to salute, to bow to.
gut, a. good, dear.
Güte, f. kindness.
gutmachen, v. a. to repair, to
redress, to make amends for.
Haar, n. hair.
halten (für), v. a. to take for, to
hold, to estimate.
Halunke, m. scamp, rascal, rogue.
Hand, f. hand.
Händel, pl. m. quarrel; — bekommen, to have a quarrel.
haſſen, v. a. to dislike, to hate.
Hauptmann, m. captain.
Hauptrolle, f. principal part.
Haus, n house.
Haushaltung, f. household.
heftig, a. violent, ardent.
heilig, a. sacred, solemn.
heimlich, adv. low, softly, secretly.
heimzahlen, v. a. to retaliate, to
give tit for tat.
Heirat, f. marriage.
heiraten, v. a. to marry.
Heiratskontrakt, m. marriage-
contract.
heiß, a. warm, hot.
heißen, v. n. to be called.
helfen, v. a. to help.
Heller, m. farthing.
heraushelfen, v. a. to help (get)
a person out of a difficulty.
herauskommen, v. n. to come
from (out).
heraussagen, v. a. to speak up (out).
hereinkommen, v. n. to enter, to
come in.

hereintreten, v. n. to enter.
herkommen, v. n. to arrive, to come here.
Herr, m. sir, master; gnädiger —, honoured sir, your honour, my lord; mein — , sir; meine —en, gentlemen.
Herrlichkeit, f. happiness.
herschicken, v. a. to send.
hervorholen, v. a. to take out of.
hervorkommen, v. n. to come on the stage.
Herweg, m. way here (hither).
Herz, n. heart; von —en, sincerely.
herzlich, a. cordial, hearty, affectionate; adv. heartily, cordially.
heute, adv. to-day.
hieher (hierher), adv. here.
hiermit, adv. herewith.
Himmel, m. heaven; barmherziger —, good heavens.
himmlisch, a. heavenly, delightful.
hinauf, adv. up.
hinausfliegen, v. n. to fly.
hindern, v. a. to hinder, to prevent.
hinter, prp. behind.
Hintergrund, m. back, background.
Hinterthür, f. back-door.
hinweg, adv. away; so — eilen, to run away so fast.
Hiob, m. Job.
Hitze, f. heat, ardour.
hm, i. hum.
hochgeneigt, a. honorable.
Hochzeit, f. wedding; zur —, auf der —, at the wedding.
Hochzeitgeschenk, n. wedding-present.
Hof, m. court; den — machen, to pay court to.
höflich, adv. courteously, politely.
holen, v. a. to take, to fetch.
holla, i. hollo, holla.
Hölle, f. hell.
hören, to hear, to listen to.
hübsch, a. pretty.
Huldigung, f. homage.

Humor, m. humour.
hundertmal, adv. a hundred times.
Ihro (Gnaden), your honour.
Ihrerseits, adv. on your part.
immer, adv. always, ever; für —, for ever.
indes, adv. meanwhile, in the mean time.
innig, adv. deeply, heartily, sincerely.
Irrtum, m. error.
ja, adv. yea, yes.
Jammer, m. grief, misfortune, pity.
jawohl, adv. yes indeed.
jeder, e, es, prn. every one.
jedermann, prn. every one, everybody.
jemand, prn. somebody.
jetzt, adv. now; eben (gerade) —, just now.
jung, a. young.
Junge, m. youth, young man.
Junggesell, m. bachelor.
Juwelier, m. jeweller.
Kabinett, n. side-room.
Kammerdiener, m. valet.
Karte, f. plan.
kaum, adv. scarcely.
Kehle, f. throat; die — abschneiden, to cut the throat.
kehren, v. a. to turn.
kein, a. not a, none.
Kerl, m. fellow.
Kind, n. child.
kitzlich, a ticklish, nice, difficult.
klatschen, v. n. to crack.
klein, a. little.
klug, a. clever.
Kommission, f. commission, charge.
Kompliment, n. compliment.
Komplott, n. conspiracy, plot.
Kopf, m. head.
Kostüm, n. uniform; costume.
krank, a. ill.
Kredit, m credit, account.
Kriegskamerad, m. brother officer, fellow-soldier.

Küche, f. kitchen.
künftig, a. future, intended.
Kurier, m. courier.
Kurierstiefel, m. jackboot.
kürzlich, adv. lately, shortly.
Kutsche, f. carriage, coach.
lachen, v. n. to laugh; (über, at).
Lage, f. situation.
Lakai, m. valet, footman, lackey.
lang, a. long.
langsam, adv. slowly.
Lärm, m. noise.
lassen, v. a. to allow, to let.
laut, a. loud, aloud.
lauter, adv. mere, pure.
leben, v. n. to live, to be alive
   (living).
Leben, n. life.
lebendig, a alive; lively.
lebhaft, a. lively, active.
legen, v. a. to put.
leicht, a. easy; adv. easily.
leichtsinnig, a. thoughtless.
leid, a. sorry; es thut (ist) mir —,
   I am sorry; einem etwas zu=
   leide thun, to do a person harm.
leiden, v. a. u. n. to suffer.
leise, adv. softly, aside.
leisten, v. a. to do, to render;
   Gesellschaft —, to bear (keep)
   company.
lesen, v. a. to read.
letzt, a. last.
leuchten, v. a. to light.
leugnen, v. a. to deny.
Leute, pl. people, servants.
L'hombre (Lomber) n. ein Karten=
   spiel. Das Wort ist spanischen
   Ursprungs und bedeutet „der
   Mann."
Licht, n. candle.
lieb, a. dear; es ist mir —, I am
   obliged (glad).
lieben, v. a to love.
liebenswürdig, a. nice, lovely,
   amiable.
lieber, adv. rather.

liebhaben, v. a. to love.
Liebhaber, m. lover.
liederlich, a. dissipated, wild;
   Bruder —, spendthrift, rake.
liegen, to lie.
link, a. left; zur Linken, on the
   left.
lösen, v. a. to unravel, to explain.
losgehen, v. n. to begin.
losmachen (sich), v. r. to get away.
Lotterbube, m. scoundrel, rascal.
Lust, f. desire, inclination.
lustig, a. amusing.
Lustspiel, n. comedy.
machen, v. a. to make, to do.
mächtig, a. mighty, powerful; able.
Mädchen, n. girl.
Mama, f. mamma.
Mann, m. husband, gentleman.
Mantel, m. cloak.
marsch, i. off, march.
Maske, f. mask.
mäßigen, v. a. to moderate.
Maßregel, f. measures, pl.
mehr, adv. more; nicht—, no longer.
Meile, f. mile.
mein, c, —, prn. my.
meinen, v. n. to think, to mean.
   es gut —, to mean well.
meinetwegen, adv. for my sake.
   for aught I care, as you like.
Mensch, m. man, gentleman.
merken, v. a. to remark.
Mietkutsche, f. hackney-coach.
Ministerium, n. ministry.
mischen (sich drein), v. r. to interfere.
mißfallen, v. n. to displease.
mißlingen, v. n. to miscarry, to
   fail.
Mißverständnis, n. misunderstanding
mitbringen, v. a. to bring (with
   one).
miteinander, adv. together, with
   one another.
mitnehmen. v. a. to take (with
   one).

mittanzen, v. n. to join in the dance.

mitteilen, v. a. to impart.

Modehändlerin, f. milliner.

mögen, v. n. to like, to wish.

möglich, a. possible.

Monat, m. month.

Morgen, m. morning; heute morgen, this morning.

morgen, adv. to-morrow.

Mühe, f. trouble, pains (pl.).

Mund, m. mouth.

Münze, f. coin.

müssen, v. n. to be obliged.

Mut, m. courage.

Mutter, f. mother.

Mütze, f. cap, bonnet.

nach, prp. after, according to, to.

nachdem, c. after.

nachgeben, v. n. to yield, to consent.

nachlaufen, v. n. to run after.

Nachricht, f. news, intelligence.

nachsinnen, v. n. to reflect, to think.

Nacht, f. night; diese —, to-night; zu — speisen, to sup.

Nachtessen, n. supper.

nahe, a. near.

nähern (sich), v. r. to approach.

Name, m. name; einerlei —n führen, to bear (to have) the same name.

Narr, m. }
Närrin, f. } fool.

närrisch, a. foolish.

natürlich, a. natural.

Nebenbuhler, m. rival.

Neffe, m. nephew.

nehmen, v. a. to take; auf sich —, to take upon one's self; übel —, to take offence (at).

Neigung, f. love, affection (for), attachment.

nennen, v. a. to call.

Nest, n. nest.

neunt, ninth.

neunzehnt, nineteenth.

nicht, adv. not; — doch, surely not.

Nichte, f. niece.

nichts, nothing; — als, nothing but.

niedergeschlagen, a. downcast, dejected.

niederschlagen, v. a. to cast down, to depress.

niedersetzen, v. a. to put down; sich —, to sit down.

niemand, no one, nobody (— als, — but).

nimmermehr, adv. never.

noch, adv. yet, still; — nicht, not yet; — nicht ganz, not quite.

Notar, m. notary.

nötig, a. necessary.

nötigen, v. a. to oblige, to compel.

notwendig, a. necessary.

nun, adv. well, why, now; — denn, well then.

nur, adv. only, but, solely.

nützlich, a. useful; — sein, to be of use (to), to serve (c. acc.)

ob, c. whether.

oben, adv. above.

Oberst, m. colonel.

Oberstlieutenant, m. lieutenant-colonel.

obgleich, c. although.

oder, c. or.

offen, adv. freely, plainly, openly.

öffentlich, a. public.

Offizier, m. officer.

ohne, prp. without.

Onkel, m. uncle.

ordentlich, a. u. adv. orderly, regular; regularly.

Order, Ordre, f. order, command.

Ordnung, f. order.

Ostindien, n. East Indies.

Paar, n. pair, couple; paar, a few.

Pächter, m. tenant.

packen, v. a. to place.

Papa, m. papa.

Partie, f. match.

Peitsche, f. whip.

Person, f. character.

Perücke, f. wig.

Petersburg, St. Petersburgh.

Pferd, n. horse.

Pflicht, f. duty.

Pförtchen, n. wicket.

Pistole, f. pistole (eine Goldmünze).

plagen, v. a. to dun, to bother, to harass, to molest.

Plan, m. plan.

Platz, m. place; —, i. make room (way).

plaudern, v. n. to blab, to talk.

plötzlich, adv. suddenly.

Polizei, f. police, police office.

Postchaise, f. post-coach.

Posten, m. sum; post, place.

Postillon (Postillion), m. } postil-
Postknecht, m. } lion.

Postpferd, m. post-horse.

Poststraße, f. high road.

Postwechsel, m. stage, change of horses.

präsentieren, v. a. to present.

pressiert, adv. quick, urgently.

Probe, f. proof.

Prügel, pl. m. stripes, lickings, ill-treatment.

Punkt, m. point; — elf Uhr, punctually at eleven.

pünktlich, a. punctual; adv. —ly.

Putzhändlerin, f. milliner, dress-maker.

Putzsachen, pl. f. dress, matters of dress.

Quiproquo (quidproquo = was für was, eins fürs andere) = Mißverständnis, Versehen, mis-take.

Quittung, f. receipt; eine — da-rüber, a receipt for it.

Rache, f. revenge.

rasend, a. mad.

Raserei. f. madness.

Rat, m. advice; — geben, to advise.

raten, v. a. to advise.

Rätsel, n. riddle.

Raufer, m. duellist, bully.

rauh, a. rude.

rechnen, v. a. (auf) to reckon on, to count on.

Rechnung, f. reckoning; sich — machen auf, to count (rekon) upon (on).

recht, a. right; adv. very; — haben, to be right.

Recht, n. right (auf on).

rechtschaffen, a. honest.

Rede, f. speech, conversation.

reden, v. a. u. n. to speak, to talk.

redlich, a. honest; adv. —ly.

Regierung, f. government.

reiben, v. a. to rub.

reichen, v. a. to hand, to present, to give.

rein, adv. quite.

Reise, f. journey, trip; eine große —, a long journey.

reisen, v. a to travel, to set out.

reißen, v. a. to tear.

reiten, v. a. u. n. to ride; to impel, to urge.

reizen, v. a. to please, to charm, to tickle.

Rendezvous, n. rendezvous, place of meeting.

retten, v. a. to save.

richtig, a. right; adv. very.

Rock, m. coat.

Rolle, f. part; die — durchführen, to play the part through.

rückgängig machen, v. a. to break off.

Rückstand, m. arrears (pl.).

rufen, v. a. u. n. to call, to cry, to exclaim.

ruhen, v. n. to rest.

ruhig, a. quiet; adv. peacefully.

rühmen (sich), v. r. to boast (of a thing).

Rußland, n. Russia.

Saal, m. drawing-room.

Sache, f. thing, matter, affair.

ſachte, adv. gently.
Sankt Petersburg, St. Petersburg.
Scene, f. scene
ſchade, i. what a pity.
ſcharf, a. strict, severe.
ſcharmant, a. charming.
ſchätzen, v. a. to value, to esteem.
ſcheiden, v. n. to part, to separate.
ſcheinen, v. n. to appear to seem.
ſchenken, v. a. to give.
Schelm, m. rogue, rascal.
Schelmſtreich, m. roguish (rascally, knavish) trick, roguery, rascality.
Scherz, m. joke: — beiſeite, joking apart, without joking.
ſcherzen, v. n. to joke.
ſchicken, v. a. to send.
Schiedsrichter, m. umpire, arbitrator.
ſchlafen, v. n. to sleep.
Schlag, m. sort, kind; Leute von meinem —, persons (gentlemen) like me; — elf Uhr, upon the stroke of eleven.
ſchlagen, v. a. to beat; ſich mit einem —, to fight (to have a duel) with one.
Schlägerei, f. duel.
Schmerz, m. sorrow, grief.
ſchmieden, v. a. to forge.
ſchneiden, v. a. to cut; Geſichter —, to make grimaces (faces).
ſchnell, a. quick; adv. quickly, fast.
ſchon, adv. already.
ſchön, a. nice, pretty.
ſchonen, v. a. to spare.
Schoß, m. lap; im — ſeiner Familie, in the bosom of his family.
Schrecken, m. fear, terror.
ſchreiben, v. a. to write (an — to).
Schreibtafel, f. tablets, pocket book.
Schreibtiſch, m. writing - desk, writing-table.
Schüchternheit, f. shyness, timidity, bashfulness, modesty.

Schuld, f. fault; Schulden, debts.
ſchuldig ſein, v. a. to owe.
Schuldigkeit, f. duty.
Schurke, m. rascal, scoundrel.
ſchütteln, v. a. to shake.
Schwager, m. brother-in-law; postillion (Akt 3, Scene 3).
ſchwatzen, v. n. to talk, to gossip, to chatter.
Schweiß, m. perspiration.
ſchwer, a. heavy; — verwundet, severely wounded; — halten, to be difficult.
ſchwermütig, a. melancholy, sorrowful, low-spirited.
Schweſter, f. sister.
Schwiegerſohn, m. son-in-law.
Schwindelkopf, m. thoughtless fellow, madcap.
ſchwindeln, v. n. es ſchwindelt mir, I feel giddy (dizzy), the world is going round with me.
ſchwören, v. a. u. n. to swear.
ſechs, six; ſechſt, sixth.
Seele, f. soul, mind.
ſehen, v. a. to see; ſieh da, behold.
ſehr, adv. much, very, highly; recht —, very much.
ſeit, adv.
ſeitdem, c. u. adv. } since.
Seite, f. side; beiſeite, aside.
ſelbſtgefällig, adv. self-complacently.
ſeltſam, a strange, singular, curious.
Sergeant, m. sergeant.
ſetzen, v. a. to put; geſetzt, suppose.
ſeufzen, v. n. to sigh.
Sicherheit, f. safety.
ſieben, seven; ſiebent, seventh.
Sieg, m. victory.
ſiegeln, v. a. to seal.
ſinnreich, a. clever, ingenious.
ſo, adv. indeed, so.
ſobald (als), c. as soon as.
ſollen, v. n. to have (to be) to; er ſoll heiraten, he is to marry (to be married).

fonderbar, a. singular, strange, curious, extraordinary.
fonst, adv. otherwise, else.
Sophie, f. Sophia.
Sorge, f. care; sei außer —n, never fear.
forgfältig, adv. carefully, cautiously.
soviel, c. as far as, as much as; — ich weiß, as far as I know.
spaßhaft, a joking, jesting.
spazieren, v. n. to take a walk.
Spazierfahrt, f. drive; excursion.
Spiel, n. game, play.
spielen, v. a. to act, to personate, to play.
spornen, v. a. to spur; gestiefelt und gespornt, booted and spurred.
spornstreichs, adv. at full speed.
spottweise, adv. ironically.
sprechen, v. n. to speak; einen —, to speak with one.
Sprung, m. leap, spring.
Staatsangelegenheit, f. state affair.
Stadt, f. town, city.
Stand, m. condition; im stande sein, to be able; zustande bringen, to bring about; zustande kommen, to take place, to come to pass.
stark, a. strong.
statt, prp. instead of; zu statten kommen, to be useful to, to help.
stattlich, a. stately.
stecken, v. a. to hide, to put; to stick.
stehen, v. n. to stay, to stand.
Stelle, f. place; auf der —, on the spot, at once, immediately, directly; von der — kommen, to get on, to make progress.
stellen, v. a. to place; sich —, to pretend.
sterben, v. n. to die.
sterblich, a. mortal; adv. mortally.
Stich, m. thrust.

still, a. quiet, still; i. hush
stillstehen, v n. to be at an end.
Stimme, f. voice.
stimmen, v. a. to bring round (over).
Stock, m. cane, stick.
Stockprügel, pl. m. cuts with a cane, stripes; licking, flogging.
stören, v. a. to disturb, to interrupt.
strafen, v. a. to punish.
Straßburg, Strasbourg.
Straße, f. street; auf der —, in the streets.
Streich, m. trick.
Streit, m. dispute.
Stube, f. room; Kinderstube, nursery.
Stunde, f. hour.
Sturmwind, m. tempest, hurricane.
stutzen, v. a. to start.
sublim, a. sublime.
suchen, v. a. to look for, to seek, to try.
Sünde, f. sin.
Tag, m. day; den ganzen —, all day.
Tante, f. aunt.
tanzen, v. n. to dance.
Taugenichts, m. good-for-nothing (worthless) fellow, scamp.
Täuschung, f. deception.
tausendmal, adv. a thousand times.
teilen, v. a. to divide, to share.
Teufel, m. devil, deuce.
Thaler, m. thaler.
thun, v. a. to do.
tief, a. deep.
Tinte, f. ink.
Tisch, m. table.
toben, v. n. to rage.
Tochter, f. daughter.
töblich, a. mortal.
toll, a. mad.
Ton, m. tone.
tot, a. dead; — schlagen, to kill, to slay.

Tracht, f. dress.
tragen, v. a. to wear; to bear.
Traum, m. dream.
trennen, v. a. to sever, to separate, to break off; sich —, to part.
Trennung, f. separation.
treten, v. n. to step; zu einem —, to step up to, to advance to.
treu, a. faithful, true.
treuherzig, adv. naïvely.
triefen, v. n. to drip.
trocken, a. cool, cold.
Trunkenbold, m. drunkard.
tüchtig, a. good, suitable.
übel, a. ill; — dran sein, to be badly off; — nehmen, to be offended at, to take offence.
über, prp. at, over.
überall, adv. all round, everywhere.
überbringen, v. a. to bring, to deliver.
überdies, adv. besides, moreover.
überlassen, v. a. to leave, to give over to.
übernehmen, v. a. to accept, to take upon one's self.
überraschen, v. a. to take by surprise.
Überraschung, f. surprise.
überzeugen, v. a. to convince.
übrig, a. over, to spare; ich habe nichts —, I have nothing to spare.
übrigbleiben, v. n. to remain over.
übrigens, adv. besides, as for the rest.
Uhr, f. clock; um sechs —, at six o'clock.
um, prp. at; c. in order that; um — willen, on account of, for the sake of.
umarmen, v. a. to embrace.
umkehren, v. n. to turn back; sich —, to turn round.
umlenken, v. a. to turn round.

umsehen (sich), v. r. to look round.
Umstand, m. circumstance.
unbedingt, a. unconditional.
unbegreiflich, a. incomprehensible, inconceivable.
unbesonnen, a. rash, thoughtless, imprudent.
Unbesonnenheit, f. act of indiscretion, stupidity, imprudence.
unendlich, a. infinite, endless.
Unglück, n. misfortune.
unglückselig, a. ill-fated, ill-starred, wretched.
Uniform, f. uniform.
Unkosten, pl. expense.
Unrecht, n. wrong.
Unruhe, f. anxiety.
unschuldig, a. innocent.
unselig, a. sinful, unfortunate.
Unsinniger, m. madman, idiot.
unterdessen, adv. in the mean time.
unterdrücken, v. a. to restrain, to suppress, to repress.
Unteroffizier, m. corporal, sergeant, non-commissioned officer.
Unterschied, m. difference.
Unterschrift, f. signature.
unterstehen (sich), v. r. to dare.
unterwegs, adv. on the way.
unterwerfen (sich), v. r. to submit.
unterzeichnen, v. a. to sign.
unumschränkt, a. unrestrained; —e Vollmacht, full(unlimited)power.
unverschämt, a. insolent; Unverschämter, rascal.
Unverschämtheit, f. impudence.
unversehens, adv. unexpectedly.
Urlaub, m. leave.
Ursache, f. reason.
veranstalten, v. a. to arrange.
Veranstaltung, f. arrangement; meine —, my doing.
verbergen, v. a. to hide, to conceal.
verbinden, v. a. to oblige; einem verbunden sein für, to be obliged to a person for.

verblüffen, v. a. to take aback, to dumbfound, to astonish, to startle, to puzzle.

verdächtig, a. suspected; sich — machen, to raise (to rouse) suspicion.

verdammt, a. confounded, cursed.

verdanken, v. a. to owe.

verdienen, v. a. to deserve.

verfluchen, v. a. to curse; verflucht, i. dash it, blow it.

verfolgen, v. a. to proceed against.

verfügen (sich), v. r. to betake one's self to.

vergeben, v. a. to pardon.

vergeblich, adv. in vain, to no purpose.

Vergebung, f. pardon, forgiveness.

vergehen, v. a. to pass away, to elapse; es vergeht ihm die Lust, he gives up the desire.

vergessen, v. a. to forget.

Vergleichung, f. comparison.

verheiraten, v. a. to give away in marriage; sich —, to marry.

verhelfen, v. n. to help, to procure.

verhüten, v. a. to prevent, to avert.

verlangen, v. a. to desire, to demand.

verlassen, v. a. to leave.

verliebt, a. in love; — sein in, to be in love with, to love (c. acc.).

verlieren, v. a. to lose.

Vermögen, n. fortune.

verneigen (sich), v. r. to make a bow; sich tief —, to make a low bow.

vernünftig, a. sensible.

verpflichten, v. a. to oblige.

verraten, v. a. to betray; sich —, to betray one's self.

verreisen, v. n. to depart, to set out, to go on a journey.

verrückt, a. crazy, deranged; cracked.

verschaffen, v. a. to procure.

verschwinden, v. n. to disappear.

verschwören, v. a. to forswear.

versichern, v. a. to assure.

Verstand, m. understanding, comprehension.

verständig, a. sensible.

Verständnis, n. understanding, intelligence.

verstecken, v. a. to hide.

verstehen, v. a. to understand; (es) versteht sich, of course.

Verstockung, f. obstinacy.

vertrauen, v. a. to confide.

Vertrauen, n. confidence.

Vertraute(r), m. confidant.

vertrinken, v. a. to spend in drink.

Verwandte(r), m relation.

Verwechselung (Verwechslung), f. confusion, exchanging, mistake.

verwenden, v. a. to use.

verwundern (sich), v. r. to wonder (to be astonished) at.

verwünschen, v. a. to curse, to confound.

verzeihen, v. a. to forgive, to pardon.

verzeihlich, a. pardonable.

Verzeihung, f. pardon.

verzögern, v. a. to stave off, to put off, to postpone.

verzweifelt, a. desperate.

Vetter, m. cousin.

vielleicht, adv. perhaps.

vier, four; viert, fourth.

vierzehnt, fourteenth.

vollkommen, adv. thoroughly, perfectly, completely

Vollmacht, f. authority, full power.

von, prp. from, by.

vor, prp. ago.

voraus, adv.; zum —, before, beforehand, in advance.

vorbehalten, v. a. to keep back; sich —, to reserve.

vorbei, adv. over.

vorbeigehen, v. n. to go by; im Vorbeigehen, as you go by.

vorbeugen, v. a. to prevent (c. acc.).
vorgeblich, a. pretended.
vorhaben, v. a. to have something before one, to intend.
vorher, adv. previously, before.
vorhin, adv. a little while ago.
vorig, a. former, same.
vorkommen, v. n. to happen, to occur.
vorn, adv. in front (of the stage).
vornehm, a. distinguished.
vornehmen, v. a. to untertake. to take in hand
Vorreiter, m. outrider.
vorſchießen, v. a. to advance (money).
Vorſchlag, m. proposal.
vorſchlagen, v. a. to propose.
vorſtellen, v. a. to personate, to represent; ſich —, to imagine, to think.
Vorteil, m. advantage.
vortrefflich, a. excellent.
Vorurteil, n. prejudice.
Wache, f. watch, guard.
wachen, v. n. to watch.
Wachslicht, n. wax-candle.
wacker, a. brave.
wagen, v. a. to risk. to venture.
Wagen, m. carriage.
Wageſtück, n. venture.
Wahl, f. choice.
wählen, v. a. to choose.
wahr, a. true, real.
während, prp. during; c. while, whilst.
wahrhaftig, adv. truly, verily, indeed.
Wahrheit. f. truth; in —, really, in truth.
wahrlich, adv. in truth.
wanken, v. a. to waver, to vacillate.
wann, c. when.
warten, v. n. to wait (auf — for).
warum, adv. why.
was, pron. what, how.
Wechſel, m. bill of exchange.

Weg, m. road.
weg, adv. away, begone.
wegen, prp. on account of, about, for.
wegſchicken, v. a. to send away.
wegwerfen, v. a. to lay aside.
Weib, n. wife.
weil, c. because.
weit, a. u. adv. far; — voneinander, apart from each other; das Weite ſuchen, to make (to be) off, to go away; to cut and run.
welcher, e, es, pron. which, what.
Welt, f. world.
wenden, v. a. to turn; ſich —, to apply (to turn) to.
wenig, a. u. adv. little; weniger, less; wenigſt, least.
wenigſtens, adv. at least.
wer, pron. who.
werden, v. n. to become (aus, of).
werfen, v. a. to throw.
Werk, n. work; ans —, to work at it.
weſentlich, a. important, material.
weswegen, adv. wherefore, for what reason.
wetten, v. a. to wager, to bet.
wichtig, a. important.
wider, prp. against; — Willen, against one's will.
widerfahren, v. n. to happen.
wie, c. as, how; adv. like.
wieder, adv. in return, again.
wiedererſcheinen, v. n. to reappear.
wiederſehen, v. a. to see again.
Wildfang, m madcap, harebrained fellow.
Willen, m. will, wish.
willkommen, a. welcome.
Winter, m. winter.
wirklich, adv. truly, really.
wirtſchaften, v. a. to manage, to behave.
Wirtshaus, n. inn, public house.
wiſſen, v. a. to know.

Witwe, f. widow.
wohin, adv. where to, whither.
wohl, adv. well, perhaps, probably.
wohnen, v. n. to live.
Wolke, f. cloud.
wollen, v. a. to like, to want.
worin, adv. wherein, in which.
Wort, n. word, promise.
Wortbrüchigkeit, f. breach of promise.
worüber, adv. whereat; — lachst du, what are you laughing at.
wozu, adv. why.
Wucherer, m. usurer.
Wunsch, m. wish, desire.
Wüstling, dissolute fellow, rake.
zählen, v. n. to rely, to reckon, to count (auf, on, upon).
Zank, m. quarrel.
zärtlich, a. tender, soft.
zehn, ten; zehnt, tenth.
Zeichen, n. sign.
Zeit, f. time.
zeitig, adv. soon, early.
Zeitverlust, m. loss of time.
Zeug, n. nonsense, rubbish.
Zeuge, m. witness.
ziehen, v. a. to draw.
ziemlich, adv. moderately; — von einem Alter sein, to be pretty much of the same age.
Zimmer, n. room.
zittern, v. n. to tremble.
Zorn, m. rage, anger.
zu, prp. at, to; — adv. too.
zudenken, v. a. to intend for, to destine for.
zuerst, adv. at first.
Zufall, m. accident.
zufrieden, a. contented, satisfied.
zugeben, v. a. to allow, to consent.
zugleich, adv. at once, at the same time.
zulegen, v. a. to assume.

zuleib thun einem etwas, to do harm to a person (to do a person harm).
zurechtsetzen, v. a. (einem den Kopf), to bring one to reason.
zurück, adv. back.
zurückbringen, v. a. to convey back.
zurückführen, v. a. to bring back.
zurückhalten, v. a. to hold back, to stop.
zurückholen, v. a. to bring back, to fetch back.
zurückkommen, v n. to return, to come back.
Zurückkunft, f. return.
zurückreisen, v. n. to return.
zurückschicken, v. a. to send back.
zurücksein, v. n. to have returned, to be back.
zusammen, adv. together.
zustoßen, v. n. to befall, to happen to.
zuvorkommen, v. n. to forestall, to anticipate, to be before-hand.
zuweisen, adv. at times, now and then, sometimes.
Zwang, m. compulsion, constraint; — anthun, to coerce, to constrain (c. acc.)
zwanzig, twenty; zwanzigst, twentieth.
zwar, adv. it is true, indeed.
zwei, two; zweit, second.
zweifach, a. double, twofold.
zweifelhaft, a. doubtful.
zweifeln, v. n. to doubt, to hesitate.
zweimal, adv. twice.
zweitausend, two thousand.
zwingen, v. a. to compel, to force.
zwischen, prp. between.
zwölf, twelve; zwölft, twelfth.

Psychology Simplified for Teachers. Gordy's well known "New Psychology." Familiar talks to teachers and parents on how to observe the child-mind, and on the value of child-study in the successful teaching and rearing of the young. With Questions on each Lesson. **$1.25.** *Twenty-second thousand!*

Page's Theory and Practice of Teaching. With Questions and Answers. Paper, **50 cts.** Cloth, **$1.00.**

Dialogues. Hinds and Noble's *new idea.* Being life-like episodes from popular authors like Stevenson, Crawford, Mark Twain, Dickens, Scott, arranged in the form of simple plays, with every detail explained as to dress, make-up, utensils. furniture, etc., for school-room or parlor. **$1.50.** *Ready in September.*

College Men's 3-Minute Declamations. Up-to-date selections from live men like Chauncey Depew, Hewitt, Gladstone, Cleveland, Pres't Eliot (Harvard) and Carter (Williams) and others. New material with vitality in it for prize speaking. *Very popular.* **$1.00.**

College Maids' 3-Minute Readings. Up-to-date recitations from living men and women. On the plan of the popular College Men's Declamations, and on the same high plane. **$1.00.**

Commencement Parts. "Efforts" for all occasions. **$1.50.**

Acme Declamation Book. *Single pieces and dialogues.* For boys and girls of all ages; all occasions. Paper, 30 cts.; cloth, 50 cts.

Handy Pieces to Speak. *Single pieces and dialogues.* Primary, 20 cts.; Intermediate, 20 cts.; Advanced 20 cts. *All three for 50 cts.*

Pros and Cons. Complete debates of the affirmative and negative of the stirring questions of the day, by A. H. Craig, author of the famous Common School Question and Answer Book, now in its 187th thousand. *A decided hit.* **$1.50.**

Smith's New Class Register. The best of record books. 50 cts.

Likes and Opposites. Hinds & Noble's new Complete Synonyms and their Opposites. **50 cts.**

Letter Writing. Hinds & Noble's new handy rules for correct correspondence. **75 cts.**

Punctuation. Hinds & Noble's new Manual. Paper, 25 cts.

New Speller. Hinds & Noble's new graded lists of 5000 words which one *must* know how to spell. **25 cts.**

Craig's Revised Common School Question Book, with Answers. Enlarged Edition, revised for 1898. **$1.50.**

How to Become Quick at Figures. Enlarged Edition. **$1.00.**

How to Prepare for a Civil Service Examination. Enlarged Edition for 1898. Revised Civil Service Rules. Full instructions for both sexes. *Has helped thousands to pass.* **50 cts.**

Bad English. Humiliating "Breaks" corrected. **30 cts.**

Composition Writing Made Easy. *Very successful.* Five Grades, viz.: A, B, C, D, E. 20 cts. each. *All five for 75 cts.*

U. S. Constitution in German, French, and English, *parallel columns*, with explanatory marginal Notes. Cloth, 50c.; paper, 25c.

Bookkeeping Blanks at 30 cts. per set. Five Blank-Books to the set. Adapted for use with any text-book—Elementary, Practical, or Common School. *Used everywhere.*—Price, 30 cts. per set.

Dictionaries: The Classic Series. Half morocco, $2.00 each.
Especially planned and carefully produced to meet the requirements of students and teachers in colleges, and high schools. Up to the times in point of contents, authoritative while modern as regards scholarship, instantly accessible in respect to arrangement, of best quality as to typography and paper, and in a binding at once elegant and durable. Size 8x5½ inches.

French-English and English-French Dictionary, 1122 pages.
German-English and Eng.-Ger. Dictionary, 1112 pages.
Italian-English and English-Italian Dict., 1187 pages.
Latin-English and English-Latin Dictionary, 941 pages.
Greek-English and English-Greek Dict., 1056 pages.
English-Greek Dictionary. Price $1.00.

Dictionaries: The Handy Series. "Scholarship modern and accurate; and really beautiful print." *Pocket edition, $1.00.*
Spanish-English and English-Spanish, 474 pages, $1.00.
Italian-English and English-Italian, 428 pages, $1.00.
New-Testament Lexicon. *Entirely new. Just published. $1.00.*
Up-to-date in every respect—typographically, and lexicographically. *Contains a fine presentation of the Synonyms of the Greek Testament, with hints on discriminating usage.*

Liddell & Scott's Abridged Greek Lexicon, $1.20.

White's Latin-English Dictionary, $1.20.

White's English-Latin Dictionary, $1.20.

White's Latin-English and Eng.-Lat. Dict., $2.25.

Completely Parsed Caesar, Book I. Each page bears *interlinear* translation, *literal* translation, parsing, grammatical references. *All at a glance without turning a leaf.* $1.50. *September.*

Caesar's Idioms. Complete, with English equivalents. **25 cts.**
Alphabetically arranged for ready reference, and enabling the pupil to acquire quickly a ready facility in solving the idioms.

Hossfeld Methods: Spanish, Italian, German, French, $1.00 *each.* Keys for each, 35 cts. Letter Writer for each, $1.00 each.

Brooks' Historia Sacra, with 1st Latin Lessons. Revised, *with Vocabulary.* **Price 50 cents.** This justly popular volume, besides the Epitome Historiæ Sacræ, the Notes, and the Vocabulary, contains 100 pages of elementary Latin Lessons, making it practicable for the teacher, without recourse to any other book, to carry the pupil quickly and in easy steps over the ground preparatory to a profitable reading of the Epitome Historiæ Sacræ.

Brooks' First Lessons in Greek, *with Lexicon.* Revised Edition. Covering sufficient ground to enable the student to read the New Testament in the Greek. **Price 50 cts.**

Brooks' New Virgil's Æneid, *with Lexicon.* Revised Edition. Notes, Critical, Historical and Mythological. Metrical Index and Map, and numerous engravings of Antique Statues, Arms, Gems, Coins and Medals. *Also Questions for Examinations.* **$1.50.**

Brooks' New Ovid's Metamorphoses, *with Lexicon.* Illustrated and Revised Edition. Expurgated and adapted for Mixed Classes. Elucidated by an Analysis and Explanation of each Table. With English Notes, Historical, Mythological and Critical, *and Questions for Examinations.* **Price reduced to $1.50.**

Hinds & Noble's Hebrew Grammar, $1.00.

Tutorial Classic Texts and Teachers' Editions—(*Continued.*)

Cæsar's Gallic War, **Book VII.**, Text and Notes, 60 cents.
Same, Teachers' Edition, with Translation, $1.00.
Cicero Ad Atticum, **Book IV.**, Text and Notes, 60 cents.
Literal Translation, with Test Papers, 50 cents.
Cicero de Amicitia, Text and Notes, 40 cents.
Same, with Test Papers, and the Vocabularies, 60 cents.
Same, Teachers' Edition, with Translation, 70 cents.
Cicero De Finibus, **Book I.**, Text and Notes, 60 cents.
Same, Teachers' Edition, with Translation, 80 cents.
Cicero De Finibus, **Book II.**, Text and Notes, 75 cents.
Literal Translation, with Test Papers, 50 cents.
Cicero De Senectute, Text and Notes, 40 cents.
Same, Teachers' Edition, with Translation, 70 cents.
Cicero In Catilinam **Book I.**, Text and Notes, 40 cents.
Same, Teachers' Edition, with Translation, 70 cents.
Cicero Pro Archia, Text and Notes, 40 cents.
Same, Teachers' Edition, with Translation, 70 cents.
Cicero Pro Balbo, Text and Notes, 40 cents
Same, Teachers' Edition, with Translation, 70 cents.
Cicero Pro Cluentio, Text and Notes, 75 cents.
Same, Teachers' Edition, with Translation, $1.20.
Cicero Pro Marcello, Text and Notes, 40 cents.
Same, Teachers' Edition, with Translation, 70 cents.
Cicero Pro Milone, Text and Notes, 75 cents.
Same, Teachers' Edition, with Translation, $1.20.
Cicero Pro Plancio, Text and Notes, 60 cents.
Cornelius Nepos, Text and Notes, 25 cents.
See Handy Literal Translation, 50 cts.; *Interlinear,* $1.50.
Demosthenes' Androtion, Text and Notes, $1.00.
Literal Translation, 50 cents.
Demosthenes' Meidias, Text and Notes, $1.30.
Literal Translation, 75 cents.
Euripides' Alcestis, Text and Notes, 70 cents.
Same, Teachers' Edition, with Translation, $1.00.
Euripides' Andromache, Text and Notes, 70 cents.
Same, Teachers' Edition, with Translation, $1.00.
Euripides' Bacchæ, Text and Notes, 75 cents.
Same, Teachers' Edition, with Translation, $1.20.
Euripides' Hippolytus, Text and Notes, 75 cents.
Same, Teachers' Edition, with Translation, $1.20.
Herodotus, **Book III.**, Text and Notes, $1.00.
Same, Teachers' Edition, with Translation, $1.40.
Herodotus, **Book VI.**, Text and Notes, 60 cents.
Same, Teachers' Edition, with Translation, $1.00.
Herodotus, **Book VIII.**, Text and Notes, 60 cents.
See, "Handy Literal Translation," 50 cents.
Homer's Iliad, **Book VI.**, Text and Notes, 40 cents.
Homer's Iliad, **Book XXIV.**, Text and Notes, 75 cents.
Homer's Odyssey, **Books IX.-X.**, Text and Notes, 60 cents.
Homer's Odyssey, **Books XI.-XII.**, Text and Notes, 60 cents.
Homer's Odyssey, **Books XIII.-XIV.**, Text and Notes, 60 cents.
Literal Trans., **Books IX.-XIV.**, *with Test Papers,* 60 cents.
Homer's Odyssey, **Book XVII.**, Text and Notes, 40 cents.
Horace's Epodes, Text and Notes, 40 cents.
See "Handy Literal Translation," 50 cts.; *"Interlinear,"* $1.50.
Horace's Odes, **Book I.**, Text and Notes, 40 cents.
Same, Teachers' Edition, with Translation, 70 cents.
Horace's Odes, **Book II.**, Text and Notes, 40 cents.
Same, Teachers' Edition, with Translation, 70 cents.
Horace's Odes, **Book III.**, Text and Notes, 40 cents.
Same, Teachers' Edition, with Translation, 70 cents.

Higher Greek Reader, The Tutorial, 60 cents.
Key to Part II. of same, 60 cents.

History: English, Roman, Grecian.

English History, Intermediate Text Book of: *A Longer History.*
  Volume I., to 1485, $1.00.
  Volume II., 1485 to 1603, $1.00.
  Volume III., 1603 to 1714, $1.00.
  Volume IV., 1714 to 1837, $1.00.
  Extra volume, 1685 to 1801, $1.00.
Synopsis English Hist., *with Test Questions:*
  1485 to 1603; 1660 to 1714; 1760 to 1798; *each* 40 cents.
Grecian History, in six Volumes.
  1. Early Grecian History, to 495 B.C., 70 cents.
  2. History of Greece, 495 to 431 B.C., 70 cents.
  3.   "   "   431 to 404 B.C., 70 cents.
  4.   "   "   404 to 362 B.C., 70 cents.
  5.   "   "   371 to 323 B.C., 70 cents.
  6. History of Sicily, 490 to 289 B.C, 70 cents.
Synopsis of Grecian History, Interleaved, *with Test Questions:*
  Part I. to 495 B.C., 25 cents.
  Part II. 495 to 404 B.C., 25 cents.
  Part III. 404 to 323 B.C., 25 cents.
  Also 405 to 358 B.C., 25 cents.
  Also 382 to 338 B C., 25 cents.
  Sicily, 490 to 289 B C., 25 cents.
Rome, The Tutorial History of, to A.D. 14, 80 cents.
Roman History, Outlines of, 55 cents.
Rome, A Longer History:
  1. 287 to 202 B.C., 80 cents.
  2. 202 to 133 B.C., 80 cents.
  3. 133 to 78 B.C., 80 cents.
  4. 78 to 31 B.C., 80 cents.
  5. 31 B.C. to 96 A.D., The Early Principate, 60 cents.
Synopsis of Roman History, Interleaved, *with Test Questions:*
  1. 202 to 133 B.C., 25 cents.
  2. 133 to 78 B.C., 25 cents.
  3. 63 B.C. to 14 A.D., 25 cents.
  4. 31 B.C. to 37 A.D. 25 cents.
  Also to 14 A.D., 25 cents.
  Also 14 to 96 A.D., 25 cents.

English Language, Literature, etc.

Low's English Language, 60 cents.
Low's Intermediate Text Book of English Literature:
  Volume I., to 1580, 80 cents.
  Volume II., 1558 to 1660, 80 cents.
  Volume III , 1660 to 1798, 80 cents.
Ayenbite of Inwyt, *A Translation by Wyatt*, 70 cents.
Dryden's Essay on Dramatic Poesy, edited by Low, 80 cents.
Havelok the Dane, *A Translation by Wyatt*, 70 cents.
Milton's Paradise Regained, edited by Wyatt, 70 cents.
Milton's Samson Agonistes, edited by Wyatt, 60 cents.
Milton's Sonnets, *with Test Questions*, edited by Masom, 40 cents.
Saxon Chronicle, 800 to 1001 A.D., *A Translation by Low*, 70 cents.
Spenser's Fairie Queene, **Bk. I.**, with Notes and Glossary, 70 cts.
Chaucer's Man of Law's Tale, 70 cents.
Chaucer's Prologue to Knight's Tale, 70 cents.
Langland's Piers Plowman, edited by Davis, $1.20.

French Grammar, Readers, etc.

French Grammar, $1.20

Preceptor's French Course, 70 cents. *Key to same*, 70 cents.
French Prose Composition, 70 cents. *Key to same*, $1.00.
French Accidence, 60 cents. *Key to same*, 70 cents.
French Syntax, 60 cents *Key to Syntax* 70 cents.
French Prose Reader, *with Vocabulary*, 60 cents.
  Key and Notes to same, 80 cents.
Advanced French Reader, 60 cents.
Higher French Reader, edited by Weekley, $1.00.
Preceptor's French Reader, 40 cents.
Bonnechose's Bertrand du Guesclin, edited by Weekley, 55 cents.
Souvestre's Le Serf, 40 cents.

Mental and Moral Science.

Mackenzie's Manual of Ethics, $1 50.
Welton's Manual of Logic, **Volume I.**, Deductive, $2.00.
Welton's Manual of Logic, **Volume II.**, Inductive, $1.60.
Questions on Logic, 70 cents. *Key to same*, 70 cents.

Mathematics and Mechanics.

Algebra, Tutorial Intermediate, $1.00.
Astronomy, Elementary Mathematical, $1.50.
Geometry, Elements of Coördinate, 80 cents. *Key to same*, $1.00.
  Worked Examples in Coörd. Geom., 60 cents.
Geometry of Similar Figures and The Plane. 70 cents.
Mechanics, Elem'y Text Book of, 80 cents.
  Key to same, $1.00.
Mechanics, Advanced, **Vol. II.**, Statics, $1.00.
Mechanics, The Preceptor's, 70 cents.
Mechanics, First Stage, 55 cents.
Mechanics of Fluids, First Stage, 55 cents.
Dynamics, Text Book of, 60 cents.
Statics, The Tutorial, $1.00.
Statics, Text Book of, 60 cents.
Hydrostatics, Elem'y Text Book of, 50 cents. *Key to same*, 55 cts.
  Worked Examples in Hydrostatics and Mechanics, 40 cents.
Euclid, **Books I-II.**, 25 cents.
Euclid, **Books I-IV.**, 70 cents.
Trigonometry, The Tutorial, $1.00.
Trigonometry, Synopsis of, *Interleaved*, 40 cents.
Mensuration of the Simpler Figures, 60 cents.

Sciences.

Biology, Text Book of, **Part I.**, $1.00.
Biology, Text Book of, **Part II.**, $1.00.
Zoology, Text Book of, $1.60.
Botany, Text Book of, $1.60.
Heat and Light, Elem'y Text Book of, $1.00.
Heat and Light Problems, *with Worked Examples*, 40 cents.
Heat, Advanced Text Book of, $1.00.
Heat, Text Book of, $1.00. Elementary Heat, 55 cents.
Light, Text Book of, $1.00. Elementary Light, 55 cents.
Sound, Text Book of, $1.00. Elementary Sound, 40 cents.
Sound, Heat, and Light, First Stage, 55 cents.
Magnetism and Electricity, Text Book of, $1.00.
Magnetism and Electricity, First Stage, 55 cents.
Chemistry, Part I., Non-Metals, $1.00. Part II., Metals, $1.00.
Chemistry, First Stage of Inorganic, 55 cents.
Chemistry, Synopsis of Non-Metallic, *Interleaved*, 40 cents.
Qualitative Analysis, Elementary, 40 cents.
Analysis of a Simple Salt, 70 cents.
Physiography, First Stage, 55 cents.
General Elementary Science, $1.00.
Chemical Analysis, Qualitative and Quantitative, $1.00.

Tutorial Classic Texts and Teachers' Editions—(*Continued.*)

Horace's Odes, **Book IV.**, Text and Notes, 40 cents.
Same, Teachers' Edition, with Translation, 70 cents.
Horace's Odes, **Books I., II., III., IV.**, Text and Notes, $1.00.
See "Handy Translation," 50 cents. "*Interlinear*," $1.50.
Horace's Satires, Text and Notes, 80 cents.
Same, Teachers' Edition, with Translation, $1.20.
Horace's Epistles, Text and Notes, 80 cents.
Same, Teachers' Edition, with Translation, $1.20.
Juvenal's Satires, **I., III., IV.**, Text and Notes, 80 cents.
Juvenal's Satires, **VIII., X., XIII.**, Text and Notes, 60 cents.
Juvenal's Satires, **XI., XIII., XIV.**, Text and Notes, 75 cents.
See "Handy Literal Translation," 50 cents.
Livy, **Book I.**, Text and Notes, 60 cents.
Same, Teachers' Edition, with Translation, $1.00.
Livy, **Book III.**, Text and Notes, 60 cents.
Same, Teachers' Edition, with Translation, $1.00.
Livy, **Book V.**, Text and Notes, 60 cents.
Same, Teachers' Edition, with Translation, $1.00.
Livy, **Book VI.**, Text and Notes, 60 cents.
Same, Teachers' Edition, with Translation, $1.00.
Livy, **Book IX.**, Text and Notes, 75 cents.
Same, Teachers' Edition, with Translation, $1.20.
Livy, **Book XXI.**, Text and Notes, 60 cents.
Same, Teachers' Edition, with Translation, $1.00.
Livy, **Book XXII.**, Chapters 1 to 51, Text and Notes, 60 cents.
Same, Teachers' Edition, with Translation, $1.00.
Ovid's Fasti, **Books III., IV.**, Text and Notes, 60 cents.
Same, Teachers' Edition, with Translation, $1.00.
Ovid's Heroides, **Books I., V., XII.**, Text and Notes, 40 cents.
Literal Translation of same, 50 cents.
Ovid's Heroides, 1, 2, 3, 5, 7, 12, Text and Notes, 70 cents.
Same, Teachers' Edition, with Translation, $1.20.
Ovid's Metamorphoses, **Book XI.**, Text and Notes, 40 cents.
Same, Teachers' Edition, with Translation, 70 cents.
Ovid's Metamorphoses, **Book XIII.**, Text and Notes, 40 cents.
Same, Teachers' Edition, with Translation, 70 cents.
Ovid's Metamorphoses, **Book XIV.**, Text and Notes, 40 cents.
Same, Teachers' Edition, with Translation, 70 cents.
Ovid's Tristia, **Book I.**, Text and Notes, 40 cents.
Same, Teachers' Edition, with Translation, 70 cents.
Ovid's Tristia, **Book III.**, Text and Notes, 40 cents.
Same, Teachers' Edition, with Translation, 70 cents.
Plato's Laches, Text and Notes, 75 cents.
Same, Teachers' Edition, with Translation, $1.20.
Plato's Phaedo, Text and Notes, 80 cents.
See "Handy Literal Translation," 50 cents.
Sallust's Catiline, Text and Notes. 60 cents.
Same, Teachers' Edition, with Translation, 90 cents.
Sophocles' Ajax, Text and Notes, 75 cents.
Literal Translation, with Test Papers, 50 cents.
Sophocles' Antigone, Text and Notes, 40 cents.
Same, Teachers' Edition, with Translation, 70 cents.
Sophocles' Electra, Text and Notes, 80 cents.
Same, Teachers' Edition, with Translation, $1.20.
Tacitus' Annals, **Book I.**, Text and Notes, 60 cents.
Tacitus' Annals, **Book II.**, Text and Notes, 60 cents.
See "Handy Literal Translation," 50 cents.
Tacitus' Histories, **Book I.**, Text and Notes, 60 cents.
Same, Teachers' Edition, with Translation, $1.00.

Terence's Adelphi, Text and Notes, 75 cents.
   See "Handy Literal Translation," 50 cents.
Thucydides, **Book I.**, Notes and Test Papers only, 40 cents.
Thucydides, **Book VII.**, Text and Notes, 60 cents.
   See "Handy Literal Translation," 50 cents.
Vergil's Eclogues, Text and Notes, 75 cents.
   Same, Teachers' Edition, with Translation, $1.20.
Vergil's Georgics, **Books I.**, **II.**, Text and Notes, 75 cents.
   Same, Teachers' Edition, with Translation, $1.20.
Vergil's Aeneid, **Book I.**, Text and Notes, 40 cents.
   Same, Teachers' Edition, with Translation, 70 cents.
   See "Handy" Translation, 50 cents; *"Interlinear,"* $1.50.
Vergil's Aeneid, **Book II.**, Text and Notes, 40 cents.
   Same, Teachers' Edition, with Translation, 70 cents.
Vergil's Aeneid, **Book III.**, Text and Notes, 40 cents.
   Same, Teachers' Edition, with Translation, 70 cents.
Vergil's Aeneid, **Book IV.**, Text and Notes, 40 cents.
   Literal Translation, 50 cents.
Vergil's Aeneid, **Book V.**, Text and Notes, 40 cents.
   Same, Teachers' Edition, with Translation, 70 cents.
Vergil's Aeneid, **Book VI.**, Text and Notes, 40 cents.
   Same, Teachers' Edition, with Translation, 70 cents.
Vergil's Aeneid, **Book VII.**, Text and Notes, 40 cents.
   Same, Teachers' Edition, with Translation, 70 cents.
Vergil's Aeneid, **Book VIII.**, Text and Notes, 40 cents.
   Same, Teachers' Edition, with Translation, 70 cents.
Vergil's Aeneid, **Book IX.**, Text and Notes, 40 cents.
Vergil's Aeneid, **Book X.**, Text and Notes, 40 cents.
   Literal Translation, Books IX-X, 50 cents.
Vergil's Aeneid, **Book XI.**, Text and Notes, 40 cents.
   Literal Translation, 50 cents.
Vergil's Aeneid, **Book XII.**, Text and Notes, 40 cents.
   Literal Translation, 50 cents
Xenophon's Anabasis, **Book I.**, Text and Notes, 40 cents.
   Same, Teachers' Edition, with Translation, 70 cents.
Xenophon's Anabasis, **Book IV.**, Text and Notes, 75 cents.
   See "Handy Literal Translation," 50 cents.
Xenophon's Cyropaedeia, **Book I.**, Text and Notes, 75 cents.
   See " Handy Literal Translation," 50 cents.
Xenophon's Hellenica, **Book III.**, Text and Notes, 80 cents.
   Same, Teachers' Edition, with Translation, $1.00.
Xenophon's Hellenica, **Book IV.**, Text and Notes, 80 cents.
   See "Handy Literal Translation," 50 cents.
Xenophon's Oeconomicus, Text and Notes, $1.00.
   Same, Teachers' Edition, with Translation, $1.40.

UNIVERSITY TUTORIAL SERIES.

Latin and Greek Texts. See above.
Latin and Greek Grammars and Readers.
   Latin Grammar, The Tutorial, 80 cents.
     Exercises to same, 40 cents. *Key to Exercises,* 70 cents.
   Latin Composition and Syntax, *with Vocabularies,* 60 cents.
     Key to same, 60 cents.
   Preceptors' Latin Course, 70 cents. *Key to same,* 70 cents.
   Latin Reader, The Tutorial, *with complete Vocabulary,* 60 cents.
     Key to Parts I., II., and V., 60 cents.
   Higher Latin Reader, $1.00. *Key to Part II. of same,* 70 cents.
   Greek Reader, The Tutorial, 60 cents.

College Men's 3=minute Declamations

$1.00—CLOTH, 381 PAGES, WITH INDEX—$1.00

Here at last is a volume containing just what college students have been calling for time out of mind, but never could find—something besides the old selections, which, though once inspiring, now fail to thrill the audience, because declaimed to death! **Live topics presented by live men! Full of vitality for prize speaking.**

Such is the matter with which this volume abounds. To mention a few names—each speaking in his well-known style and characteristic vein :

Chauncey M. Depew	President Eliot (*Harvard*)
Abram S. Hewitt	George Parsons Lathrop
Carl Schurz	Bishop Potter
William E. Gladstone	Sir Charles Russell
Edward J. Phelps	President Carter (*Williams*)
Benjamin Harrison	T. De Witt Talmage
Grover Cleveland	Ex-Pres. White (*Cornell*)
General Horace Porter	Rev. Newman Smyth
Doctor Storrs	Emilio Castelar

Here, too, sound the familiar voices of George William Curtis, Lowell, Blaine, Phillips Brooks, Beecher, Garfield. Disraeli, Bryant, Grady, and Choate. Poets also :—Longfellow, Holmes, Tennyson, Byron, Whittier, Schiller, Shelley, Hood, and others.

More than a hundred other authors besides! We have not space to enumerate. But the selections from them are all just the thing. And all the selections are brief.

In addition to a perspicuous list of contents, the volume contains a complete general index by titles and authors; and also a separate index of authors, thus enabling one who remembers only the title to find readily the author, or who recalls only the author to find just as readily all of his selections.

Another invaluable feature :—Preceding each selection are given, so far as ascertainable, the vocation, the residence, and the dates of birth and death of the author ; and the occasion to which we owe the oration, or address, or poem.

Like the companion volume, College Girls' Readings, this work contains many "pieces" suitable both for girls and boys, and the two books may well stand side by side upon the shelf of every student and every teacher, ever ready with some selection that is sure to please, and exactly suited to the speaker and to the occasion.

HINDS & NOBLE

4-5-13-14 Cooper Institute   New York City

Schoolbooks of all publishers at one store

A Text-Book on Letter-Writing

CLOTH—75 cents Postpaid—165 PAGES

Believing that the social and business career of our youth demands that as much attention should be bestowed upon Letter-Writing in our schools, as upon Grammar, Orthography, Penmanship, and other elementary studies, we have published a text-book showing the correct structure, composition, and uses of the various kinds of letters, including business letters. There have been added classified lists of abbreviations, foreign words and phrases most frequently used; and important postal information.

Our endeavor has been not only to produce just the book to guide the youth and the adult in social correspondence and the business man in commercial letter-writing, but also to provide the teacher with a text-book that can with confidence be placed in the hands of the pupils, boys and girls, to be studied by them like a text-book on any other subject for class recitations. That our book has been carefully planned for this purpose, and the matter conveniently arranged for class-room work, the following list of the CONTENTS bears evidence :

Part I.—LETTERS, NOTES, AND POSTAL CARDS.

KINDS OF LETTERS. Social, Domestic, Introductory; Business, Personal, Official; Miscellaneous; Public. or Open. Postal Cards.

STRUCTURE OF LETTERS. Materials; The Heading. The Introduction, The Body, The Conclusion, Folding, The Superscription, The Stamp. Type-writer Correspondence.

THE RHETORIC OF LETTERS. General Principles, Special Applications. Style and Specimens of Social Letters; of Business Letters; of Notes.

Part II.—ORTHOGRAPHY AND PUNCTUATION.

RULES. For Forming Derivatives, etc.; For Capitals; For Punctuation; Special Rules.

Part III.—MISCELLANEOUS.

Classified Abbreviations; Foreign Words, Phrases; Postal Information.

To teachers we will send postpaid at 20% discount one examination copy with a view to introduction, if this leaflet is enclosed with the order.

HINDS & NOBLE, Publishers of

How to Punctuate Correctly, Price 25c.
Likes and Opposites (Synonyms and Antonyms), Price 50c.
Composition Writing Made Easy, Price 75c.
Bad English, Price 30c.

4-5-13-14 Cooper Institute, New York City.

Schoolbooks of all publishers at one store.

NEW DIALOGUES AND PLAYS

PRIMARY—INTERMEDIATE—ADVANCED

Adapted from the popular works of well-known authors by

BINNEY GUNNISON

Instructor in the School of Expression, Boston: formerly Instructor in Elocution in Worcester Academy and in the Brooklyn Polytechnic Institute

Cloth, 650 Pages   -   -   -   Price, $1.50

Too many books of dialogues have been published without any particular reference to actual performance on platform or stage   There are no suggestions of stage business; the characters neither enter nor leave; while the dialogue progresses. no one apparently moves or feels emotion. Nothing is said at the beginning of the dialogue to show the situation of the characters, no hints are given as to the part about to be played   In plays, as ordinarily printed, there is very little to show either character or situation— all must be found out by a thorough study of the play   This may be well for the careful student. but the average amateur has no time. and often only little inclination. to peruse a whole play or a whole novel in order to play a little part in an entertainment.

Perhaps the strongest feature of our book is the carefully prepared introduction to each dialogue   Not only are the characters all named in order of importance, but the characteristics, the costumes, the relation of one to another, age, size, etc . are all mentioned   Most important of all is what is called the "Situation." Here the facts necessary to a clear comprehension of the dialogue following are given very concisely, very briefly. but it is hoped, adequately for the purpose in hand   The story previous to the opening of the dialogue is related : the condition of the characters at the beginning of the scene is stated ; the setting of the platform is carefully described.

There has been no book of dialogues published containing so much of absolutely new material adapted from the best literature and gathered from the most recent sources—this feature will be especially appreciated

May we send you a copy for inspection subject to your approval ?

HINDS & NOBLE

Publishers of 3·Minute Declamations for College Men
3-Minute Readings for College Girls Handy Pieces to Speak
Acme Declamation Book Pros & Cons (Complete Debates)
Commencement Parts (Orations. Essays, Addresses), Pieces for Prize
Speaking Contests (in press)

4-5-13-14 Cooper Institute   New York City

Books for your Library

No Private School, High School or College Library is complete without having on its shelves one or more of the following books for its students to refer to.

Teachers are ordering many of these books for their own personal use.   Notice particularly the starred (*) lines.

*Pros and Cons (Both Sides of Important Questions Discussed).....$1.50
*Three Minute Declamations for College Men...................... 1.00
*Three Minute Readings for College Girls........... .. .. 1.00
*Mackenzie's Manual of Ethics................................... 1.50
*Gordy's New Psychology 1.25
*Classic French-English, English-French Dictionary 2.00
*   "   German-English, English-German Dictionary............ 2.00
*   "   Italian-English, English-Italian Dictionary............ 2.00
*   "   Latin-English, English-Latin Dictionary......... .... 2.00
*   "   Greek-English, English-Greek Dictionary................ 2.00
*Handy Spanish-English, English-Spanish Dictionary 1.00
*   "   Italian-English, English-Italian Dictionary 1.00
 White's Latin-English Dictionary................................ 1.20
        "   English-Latin Dictionary...............................· 1.20
        "   Latin-English, English-Latin Dictionary.............. ... 2.25
*Hinds & Noble's New Testament Lexicon......................... 1.00
*Greek-English Interlinear New Testament, with Lexicon....... .. 4.00
*Hebrew-English Interlinear Old Testament, Vol. 1, Gen. and Ex. 4.00
 Craig's Revised Common School Question Book with Answers.... 1.50
 Constitution of the U. S. in German, French and English.........   .50
 Bad English Corrected..   .30
 How to Become Quick at Figures................................. 1.00
*How to Punctuate Correctly.....................................   .25
*Hinds & Noble's New Letter Writer...............................   .75
*Likes and Opposites (Synonyms and Antonyms).................   .50

We will send postpaid, subject to your approval, any of the books on this list upon receipt of the price, or if you have any school or college books, new or second-hand, which you would like to send us in exchange, we will accept them in payment, provided they are kinds we can use. Mention "The Library" when you write us.

HINDS & NOBLE,

4-5-13-14 Cooper Institute,   New York City.

College Girls'
Three-minute Readings

Here is a volume for American girls by American women—an ideal long in demand, now realized for the first time. In this book patriotism is the keynote dominating a series of new, fresh, *speakable* selections, pathetic, humorous, descriptive, oratorical; running, in fact, the gamut of the emotions. A book for the American girl and the American young woman in the college, the high school, the academy, and *the home.*

This new book is new in every sense of the word, but particularly in voicing the golden thoughts of scores of the *living* representative women of America—women educators, women philanthropists, women reformers.

Here is a *partial* list of the contributors:

Mrs. A. Giddings Park	"Susan Coolidge"
Eva Lovett Cameron (*Brooklyn Eagle*)	Agnes E. Mitchell
Edith M. Thomas	Rev. Anna H Shaw
Emma Lazarus	Margaret Junkin Preston
Ad ›laide Procter	Amelia Barr
Cel a Thax'er	Norah Perry
Christina Rossetti	Alice Cary
Anna Robertson Lindsay	Adeline Whitney
J. Ellen Foster	Emily Warren
Margaret E. Sangster	Lucy Larcom
Clara Barton	Ella Wheeler Wilcox
Frances E. Willard	Harriet Beecher Stowe
Kate Doug as Wigg'n	Mary Mapes Dodge
Isabel A Mallon (*Ladies' Home Journal*)	"Gail Hamilton"

and there are many others.

A brief note, happily worded, conveying information not to be found elsewhere, regarding the author or the occasion, accompanies most of the selections.

Teachers will find selections appropriate to Memorial Day, Arbor Day, Washington's Birthday. and all other patriotic occasions. And from the pages of this book speak the voices of many of our presidents. from Washington to McKinley.

Besides a perspicuous list of contents, the volume contains a complete general index by titles and authors; and also a separate index of authors, thus enabling one who remembers only the title to find readily the author, or who recalls only the author to find just as readily all of her selections.

Like the companion volume, College Men's Declamations, this work contains many "pieces" suitable both for girls and boys, and the two books may well stand side by side upon the shelf of every student and every teacher, ever ready with some selection that is sure to please, and exactly suited to the speaker and to the occasion.

HINDS & NOBLE, Publishers

4-5-13-14 Cooper Institute   New York City

Interlinear Scriptures

New Testament, Complete

The standard Greek text, with a new Literal Translation interlined; The King James Version in the margins; and with footnotes on the various disputed readings of the originals. *New Edition,* with a complete and entirely new Greek-English New Testament Lexicon and the Greek Testament Synonyms. Price, Cloth, $4.00; Half-leather, $5.00; Divinity Circuit, $6.00.

Old Testament, Volume I

Genesis and Exodus. The Hebrew text with Literal Translation interlined; the King James Version in left-hand margin; Revised Version in right-hand margin; and with footnotes on the various disputed readings of the originals. This volume also contains the Hebrew alphabet with the English equivalents, and tables showing the variations of the Hebrew verb. Price, Cloth, $4.00; Half-leather, $5.00; Divinity Circuit, $6.00.

New Testament Lexicon

(separate). To satisfy the demand of those who have already purchased the previous edition of the Interlinear New Testament without the Lexicon, and for the convenience of those who want a strictly authoritative handy Lexicon to refer to, we have published the Greek-English New Testament Lexicon separate—two styles—handy-volume s i z e, bound in cloth; and large-paper size in sheets to bind up with previous edition of the Interlinear New Testament. Price, $1.00, either style.

Any of the above books will be sent postpaid upon receipt of the price.

HINDS & NOBLE

4, 5, 13, 14, Cooper Institute, New York City